FELIZ NAUGHTY DOG

THE DOGMOTHERS - BOOK SEVEN

roxanne st. claire

Feliz Naughty Dog
THE DOGMOTHERS BOOK SEVEN

ISBN Print: 978-1-952196-15-7
ISBN Ebook: 978-1-952196-14-0

COVER DESIGN: The Killion Group, Inc.
INTERIOR FORMATTING: Author E.M.S.

Critical Reviews of
Roxanne St. Claire Novels

"Non-stop action, sweet and sexy romance, lively characters, and a celebration of family and forgiveness."
— *Publishers Weekly*

"Plenty of heat, humor, and heart!"
— *USA Today* (Happy Ever After blog)

"Beautifully written, deeply emotional, often humorous, and always heartwarming!"
— *The Romance Dish*

"Roxanne St. Claire is the kind of author that will leave you breathless with tears, laughter, and longing as she brings two people together, whether it is their first true love or a second love to last for all time."
— *Romance Witch Reviews*

"Roxanne St. Claire writes an utterly swoon-worthy romance with a tender, sentimental HEA worth every emotional struggle her readers will endure. Grab your tissues and get ready for some ugly crying. These books rip my heart apart and then piece it back together with the hope, joy and indomitable loving force that is the Kilcannon clan."
— *Harlequin Junkies*

"As always, Ms. St. Claire's writing is perfection...I am unable to put the book down until that final pawprint the end. Oh the feels!"
— *Between My BookEndz*

Before
The Dogmothers...
there was

Sit...Stay...Beg (Book 1)
New Leash on Life (Book 2)
Leader of the Pack (Book 3)
Santa Paws is Coming to Town (Book 4 – a Holiday novella)
Bad to the Bone (Book 5)
Ruff Around the Edges (Book 6)
Double Dog Dare (Book 7)
Bark! The Herald Angels Sing – (Book 8 – a Holiday novella)
Old Dog New Tricks (Book 9)

Find information and buy links for all these books here:
http://www.roxannestclaire.com/dogfather-series

For a complete guide to all of the characters in both The Dogfather and Dogmothers series, see the back of this book. Or visit www.roxannestclaire.com for a printable reference, book lists, buy links, and reading order of all my books. Be sure to sign up for my newsletter to find out when the next book is released! And join the private Dogfather Facebook group for inside info on all the books and characters, sneak peeks, and a place to share the love of tails and tales!

www.facebook.com/groups/roxannestclairereaders/

Chapter One

Pru stared at the text message on her phone, a ribbon of disappointment curling through her.

"Seriously, Emma?" she murmured, falling back against the Buick's back seat as she ripped the wrapper off a mini candy cane that was about to become breakfast and comfort food all in one peppermint sugar bomb. "Way to steal my Christmas Eve joy."

Instantly, Gala, the dachshund sitting on Gramma Finnie's lap in the passenger seat, turned and gave her a sad look that reflected exactly how Pru felt.

"Is there a problem, lass?" Gramma Finnie asked, stroking Gala's tan head. "Are we running late for your meeting? Traffic is heavy in Bitter Bark today."

"Oh, no, we're right on time for the team kickoff in Bushrod Square. It's just...other stuff." Vague, but easier than trying to explain to her great-grandmother why this news was such a drag.

"Donchya be worryin', dear Prudence," she cooed in her lilting brogue. "I find it hard to believe you've left a single stone unturned organizin' the Random Acts of Christmas Kindness for Bitter Bark High.

Look at that bag full of instructions and lists and other RACK goodies to help your school win."

"Win." Pru grinned and slurped the candy cane. "And eat."

Gramma laughed. "General Pru's got this." She winked as she said the nickname their family had been calling Pru forever. "I've no doubt Bitter Bark High will beat the other schools in the county by RACKing up the most points."

Pru let out a sigh and threw a look at her backpack, which was, as her great-grandmother had correctly noted, a General Prudence Kilcannon Bancroft special. Maybe if the general spent less time managing college résumé-building projects like RACK IT UP and more time flirting with guys on the basketball team, she'd have a boyfriend for her team partner today, like Emma did.

"I guess." Pru sucked the candy to a sharp point and tunneled her free hand into the fat rolls on Pyggie's neck, Yiayia's other doxie, who was curled next to her in the back seat. "But it's never fun to get ditched for boys."

"What do you mean?" Yiayia, the Greek grandmother who'd come into their extended family a few years ago, took her gaze off town traffic long enough to eye Pru in the rearview mirror.

"Emma and Charlotte were supposed to be my RACK IT UP partners today," Pru explained. "And I made us the absolute most amazing list of Random Acts of Christmas Kindness, too." And maybe overdecorated it just a bit. "But Emma just texted me that they want to partner with their boyfriends today." She rolled her eyes. "So I'm flying solo."

"That's a random act of Christmas *un*kindness, if you ask me," Yiayia said. "Is there anything worse than picking a man over a friend on Christmas Eve?"

"Nothing," Gramma Finnie said with a sideways look at Yiayia. "Unless it's dragging your friend along to shop for one *on Christmas Eve.*"

Pru frowned at the puzzling comment, but then another text came in from Emma.

You're not mad, right? We figured since you're running the show you can get another team. Or come with us, of course!

"Just what I want to be, a fifth wheel." She thumbed back a quick, *No problem! You guys have fun!* and tossed the phone on top of her bag, pushing down her growing resentment.

"There *are* no other teams," she said, more to herself than the grannies. "And now I'll have to do my random acts alone, on foot, since Emma was going to drive. We were going to take Linda May's raspberry croissants to the Starling Senior Living Center." She made a face. "Now they'll have all the fun of handing them out to the seniors *and* get any extra croissants."

"Doesn't really matter as long as your school 'racks' up the points, right?" Gramma Finnie asked, always seeing the silver lining in any dark cloud. "The more points, the more chance you have of Bitter Bark High winning."

"True." Pru grabbed her phone and checked the RACK IT UP app. "In Vestal Valley County, it's still a three-way tie between Holly Hills, Bitter Bark, and Sweetheart Springs, which is a shock considering how little interest my whole school has in this. But they'll all want the prize."

Most of her friends acted like participating in Random Acts of Christmas Kindness was totally bogus and dumb, but they'd all be first in line if Bitter Bark won an all-expenses-covered Winter Formal with DJ Fearsome McQ.

"Did you say Sweetheart Springs?" Yiayia asked, her dark brows rising with surprise.

"Right? A dark horse for sure," Pru said, thumbing through the list of participating high schools on the app. "I expected Holly Hills High would crush this, since they are the town that Christmas built, and Sweetheart Springs is full of wedding parties and honeymooners. Oh, and rich people who own second homes. The high school isn't exactly famous for its spirit. But the judges gave some kids forty points for painting a Christmas mural on the side of a foster home overnight in freezing weather." She let out an exasperated sigh. "Why didn't I think of that?"

"That's close to the mall where we're going after we drop Pru off, isn't it?" Yiayia said under her breath to Gramma Finnie.

Gramma Finnie nodded, but added a warning look.

"Where exactly are you two going after you drop me off?" Pru asked, eyeing the octogenarians, and getting a whiff of...trouble.

"Nowhere."

"Not important, lass."

A zing shot through her at the dismissive responses. "Is this Dogmothers business that you forgot to tell *me*, the honorary member of your matchmaking team? Are you working on Ella's match?" Her voice rose with enough excitement for Pyggie to force himself up, nearly taking a lick of the dagger-sharp candy cane Pru pointed

4

at the front seat as she demanded to know more. "Are you getting her some of that famous hot springs water that's supposed to make you fall in love, hence the unfortunate name of the town Sweetheart Springs?"

"Settle down, Prudence," Yiayia said quickly. "There's no matchmaking happening."

Gramma Finnie lifted a dubious brow, silent.

"What?" Yiayia shot back. "I have an errand to run at the mall is all, which happens to be right between Holly Hills and Sweetheart Springs."

"You're going to the Vestal Village Mall on Christmas Eve? With the dogs?" Pru asked.

"Oh, dogs are more than welcome," Yiayia said. "They're trying to cash in on Bitter Bark's huge tourist success by letting dogs go everywhere, so Pyggie and Gala will be safe and happy."

"But will *you*?" Pru asked. "That place'll be a madhouse today what with that massive Santa's Workshop and the indoor train and carolers everywhere. Who in their right mind would go there on Christmas Eve?" Let alone two octogenarians and their dachshunds.

Once again, an indecipherable look passed between the two women, a look that Pru ached to interpret. Few things were as fun as the grannies on a matchmaking mission.

"What are you going to get?" Pru asked.

"Caught," Gramma Finnie whispered. "Then killed."

"*Excuse me*?" Pru launched forward to put her face between them. "What are you talking about?"

Yiayia gave an exasperated sigh. "It's Christmas Eve, Prudence. There have to be *some* secrets."

"From *me*?"

Gramma Finnie tsked. "You just concern yourself with racking up points today."

"Racking them up *alone*," she murmured, remembering her plight.

"Well, this is a Christmas thing," Yiayia told her. "Don't you want a surprise under the tree?"

"Yeah, and maybe he'll be cute and ask me to the Winter Formal I'm working my butt off to win for the school." She dropped back in her seat with a huff.

"You could partner up with someone who doesn't have a team yet," Gramma Finnie suggested. "And *that* could be your first Random Act of Christmas Kindness, lass."

"I don't get RACK points for that."

Gramma looked over her bifocals at Pru. "Then perhaps you're missing the *point* of Christmas kindness," she reminded her gently.

"Sorry." Pru held up a hand, acknowledging the admonishment. "Everyone has a partner, Gramma. I made sure of that."

"What about him?" Yiayia pointed to a kid on the sidewalk in front of town hall. "Maybe that boy needs a partner, other than that horse he's with."

Pru snorted at the comment and the absurd suggestion. "That's a greyhound, Yiayia, and that's no *boy*. That's the new kid from California. He's not on the list today, so no worries that he'll be looking for a partner. I doubt very much Lucas Darling is on his way to the RACK IT UP kickoff in the square."

Not to mention that he was the very last person on earth Pru would want as a partner. Unless she longed to spend the day with a broody, moody loner who hadn't said two words to anyone at school since he'd arrived as a transfer student a few weeks ago in the middle of the semester.

"He's a good-looking fella," Gramma Finnie commented as Yiayia slowed the car at the Ambrose Avenue intersection in the heart of town, a few feet from where Lucas and his dog stood. "If you like a man who's Gregory Peck meets Tony Curtis with a little James Dean on the side."

Pru almost choked on candy cane-flavored saliva. "Jimmy Dean? Like the sausage?"

Yiayia barked a laugh, and Gramma Finnie just shook her head. "Makes you feel old, doesn't it, Agnes?"

"Speak for yourself, Finola," Yiayia replied, never one to admit her age under any circumstances.

But Pru ignored the grannie banter for a moment to study Lucas and the chocolate and white greyhound who pranced next to him. She might not know who Peck or Dean or...*whoever* was, but she got what Gramma Finnie was saying.

The talk, dark, smoldering bad boy was universal and ageless in his appeal, a high school cliché no matter what year the class graduated. And Lucas Darling owned the part right down to the leather jacket with some just-a-little-too-long black hair over the collar. All those types looked hot in jeans and somehow carried off a jawline that could slice something. They never smiled, they never made eye contact, and when they liked a girl...well, she wasn't the girl who organized volunteer projects so the winning school could have a dance with a professional DJ.

And the fact that he had that super cool dog? Just made him more mysterious and attractive.

Nope, a guy like that wouldn't be caught dead in a tux at the Winter Formal.

"Rumors swirl around him like storm clouds," Pru told them. "Some kids say he's from a big Hollywood family who disowned him. Or that he did something so bad his only choice was Bitter Bark or juvie, so he had to move here and live with his aunt. Oh, there's also the one that he's the secret love child of an aging rock star. Take your pick, ladies. There's no shortage of folklore surrounding Bitter Bark's newest and most enigmatic arrival."

"Don't believe everything you hear about a person," Yiayia said as she turned into the parking lot behind the bookstore, the lot only locals knew about. "Rumors aren't always true."

Gramma shrugged. "There's a kernel of truth in every lie," she said.

"Gramma Finnie," Pru said on a surprised laugh. "Not like you to take the less-than-positive side."

"I'm just sayin', lass. Some people are fundamentally *not* good."

Before Pru could respond, stunned into momentary silence by the out-of-character comment, Yiayia threw the car into park and sliced Gramma with a dark look.

"Finola Kilcannon, you just stop it now. You don't know anything about him. You are basing this on hearsay and gossip, and I am sick of it."

Pru inched back at the passion in her voice. "Wow, Yiayia. You really believe in that boy." The old Greek grandmother had softened from the sarcastic fault-finder she'd been when she first moved to town, but this switch between the two best grannie friends was downright shocking.

The two ladies stared at each other, silent, while Gala lifted her little tan head and growled, sensing the tension.

"I am telling you, he's no good," Gramma Finnie ground out.

"I'm telling you I think he deserves a chance."

Pru's frown deepened. "And I'm telling you he's in my English lit class, if you want my opinion."

Finally, they turned. "We're not talkin' about your friend, lass," Gramma said.

"But you're a smart cookie, and you'd figure that out in a minute."

She opted not to correct the *your friend* part, too fascinated by the conversation. "Then who are you fighting about?"

"We're not fighting," they said in perfect unison.

"Well, you're not agreeing. Want to let me be the referee here?"

Gramma Finnie crossed her arms and looked forward, her crinkly little jaw tight as she battled whatever it was she wanted to say. Yiayia let out a sigh, her much-less-crinkled—thanks to Botox— expression looking far too serious for Christmas Eve.

"There's a man," Yiayia finally said. "I have been texting him ever since we met on Single 'n' Silver."

Pru blinked, this news almost too much to comprehend. "You've been on a dating site?"

"You don't have to sound so shocked," Yiayia fired back. "I'm old, not dead."

"No, but...wow." Her fingers literally itched to grab her phone and share this news with the massive Kilcannon-Mahoney-Santorini clan, especially her mother. "So, what's the problem with him?"

"There is no problem," Yiayia said. "He's a perfectly nice eighty-year-old man with grown children and grandchildren, and he happens to be playing Santa at the Vestal Village Mall today, and we're going to..." She swallowed. "Check him out in person before I agree to have lunch with him."

Pru drew back. "You two are going to creep on some dude dressed as Santa at the mall?" She pressed her hand to her chest, disappointment stabbing at her. "*Without* me?"

That made them both laugh a little and broke the tension.

"What don't you like about him, Gramma Finnie?" Pru asked.

"He's a mobster."

"*What?*"

"That's ridiculous." Yiayia tapped Gramma Finnie's arm lightly. "He ran a landscaping company in Sweetheart Springs for decades, and now his sons own it, and his grandchildren work there. Does that sound like Tony Soprano to you?"

"Seamus knew him," Gramma Finnie said, referring to her late husband. "And he heard all the talk."

"*Talk.*" Yiayia spat the word. "All because the man has an Italian last name. Have you ever heard anything so wrong and judgmental, Pru?"

Not from Gramma Finnie. "So, you're interested in someone who's not Greek, Yiayia?" This could be the most stunning news of all.

"Italy is a neighbor to Greece. We're all Mediterranean."

A stretch for a woman who named her dogs

Pygmalion and Galatea and believed Greece was not only the birthplace of civilization, but the center of the world. "What's his name?" she asked.

"Aldo Fiore." Just saying it brought a smile to Yiayia's lips. "Isn't it poetic?"

"If you like Mafia movies," Gramma Finnie muttered.

"Fiore means flower," Yiayia added. "Isn't that perfect for a man who spent his life growing gardens?"

"Unless someone finds themselves six feet under his rosebushes," Gramma Finnie added.

"Are you *jealous*, Gramma Finnie?" It was the only explanation, since Pru could count on one hand the times she'd ever heard her beloved great-grandmother say anything negative about anyone on the earth. If she did, it was most likely cloaked in an Irish proverb about sinners and saints and luck and love.

"Nonsense, lass. I'm protective, is all. Agnes is a woman of some means, and I don't want to see her...hurt."

Agnes Santorini might not be dead broke, but she certainly wasn't a "woman of some means." And hurt? Pru pitied the poor guy who got sliced by that steel-edged tongue.

For her part, Yiayia just lifted a carefully filled-in brow. "You were right the first time, Pru. She's jealous that I found a man and she didn't. Not unlike how you feel about your friends spending the day with their boyfriends."

"I'm not..." Pru's voice faded. Yeah, she was jealous.

But Gramma Finnie shook her head hard enough to flutter her soft white hair. "Agnes! That's not fair. I just don't want you gettin' involved with a man who could break your heart."

"I'm too smart to have my heart broken," Yiayia declared. "But I don't want life to pass me by without remembering the feeling of holding a man's hand as we step out for a date. Or his lips on mine at the end of the evening. Is that so wrong?"

When Gramma didn't answer, Yiayia turned to Pru. "Is it?" she demanded.

"I wouldn't mind a date and a kiss," Pru agreed, having reached sixteen without having either one, though she was too ashamed to say that out loud. "But what I *do* mind is you two fighting. This is killing me."

The two grannies looked at each other, sighing deeply.

"And you know what else I can't take?" Pru asked. "The idea that you would go on this Christmas Eve adventure and not take me along!"

"But you have to do Random Acts of Christmas Kindness, lass," Gramma Finnie said. "This RACK project is too important to you. You've worked so hard on all the details, and it's the last day. Points are tallied tonight at midnight."

"And we don't know Aldo's Santa schedule," Yiayia added. "We were just going to pretend to be shoppers and see if we can watch him in action with the kids."

"You can tell a lot about a man by how he interacts with children," Gramma Finnie said.

"And if he makes them an offer they can't refuse." Pru poked Yiayia playfully.

But Yiayia wasn't laughing. "I need you on my side, Prudence."

"There aren't sides," Pru said, gathering up her bag. "But you do need a cool head on this mission. I can easily do my random acts all over the mall. I get to spend Christmas Eve with my favorite Dogmothers—and pups." She gave the doxies some head rubs. "And I don't have to see half of Bitter Bark High hooked up with the other half."

"Are you sure?" Yiayia asked.

"We won't kill each other, lass."

"You might. Just let me make my speech to the kids who are in the square and make sure they understand the rules and know exactly how to send their pictures to the judges using the app or we won't get points. If you guys run the registration table, you can check off the teams as they arrive. Oh, and give everyone a list of suggested acts, because they're all too lame or in love to figure them out for themselves. Then we can head on over to Vestal Village Mall for some Santa stalking."

"And that's why they call her General Pru," Yiayia said, lifting her knuckles for a three-way fist bump.

And just like that, Pru forgot her disappointment. Who needed a boyfriend when she had the world's most fun grannies and a clandestine adventure on Christmas Eve?

Chapter Two

"You got yourself a fine great-granddaughter," Agnes said as she laid out the list of RACK teams Pru had given them, settling in at the registration table and pulling her jacket a little tighter against the cold.

"She's a good lass." Finnie straightened a pile of papers that said *Suggested Random Acts of Christmas Kindness...RACK UP POINTS!* at the top. "I'm glad she's coming with us today."

"You'd think she'd want to spend the day with kids her own age," Yiayia mused, nodding to acknowledge a family as they walked through the festive archways topping the square's entrance, two children with them running to greet the elves around Santa's sleigh. "But she always puts family first."

"That's how she was raised." Finnie took off her glasses and found a hankie in her coat pocket, taking a swipe over each lens. "The whole Kilcannon clan is a family-first group, and I believe that's something to be admired."

"True enough, but a girl that young and pretty should have some fun, not babysit a couple of crazy old grandmothers. Not that I'm old." Agnes slipped her phone from her bag and tapped the screen, then scrolled, squinting at the blurry words.

"But you are crazy. Here." Finnie held out her glasses. "Since you *are* old and too vain to wear your own."

"I only need them for reading."

"Then just look through the bottom part, and it'll help you find…who you're looking for."

Agnes took the glasses with a smile. "How do you know I'm looking for him?"

"Because it's all you've done for a week since that thing first dinged with a match."

"So shoot me for getting a little happy, Finnie. Oh, look, he changed his Single 'n' Silver picture to one of him in his Santa costume." She angled the phone. "Does he look like John Gotti to you?"

"All he needs are some prison stripes." Finnie's eyes danced with mirth just as two high school girls stopped by the table and asked for the RACK suggestions.

"I'll just need to check off your names, lassies." Finnie reached for the list of participants with one hand and held her other out to Agnes. "Glasses, please."

"Claire Cunningham and Mira Saylor," one of the girls said.

With a reluctant sigh, Agnes handed the glasses to Finnie. There'd be plenty of time later to study Aldo Fiore. As Finnie looked down the list of names, Agnes offered one of the suggestion sheets to the girls.

But they were riveted on something—or some*one*—across the square.

15

"Look at him," one of them said. "Lucas Darling. And he sure is."

"He looks like he might just take a bite of you, if you get my drift," the other mused.

Agnes studied their expressions, which looked a lot like Pyggie and Gala when the treat bag crunched, then she followed their gazes and saw long hair and a leather jacket.

"Greyhounds don't usually bite," she said with a tease in her voice.

They both turned and stared at her with that sullen, disconnected, humorless look teenagers sometimes had. Not Pru, of course, but so many of her peers. No wonder Pru would rather spend the day with old ladies. At least they had a sense of humor.

"I found you, lassies," Finnie announced. "Claire and Mira. Now take a sheet of suggestions and go RACK UP POINTS!"

One of them almost smiled. Almost. And the other fake-smiled. "You must be Pru's grandmother," she said.

"Great-grandmother," she corrected. "How did you know?"

They just exchanged a quick, silent look and then both looked off to their left, where Pru was standing on a park bench shouting out instructions to a group of kids like a cheerleader trying to drum up enthusiasm with the losing crowd. "Just a guess."

She started to walk away, but the other grabbed her arm, pointing at the list of teams. "I can read upside down," she hissed. "And he's not on there, Mira."

"No surprise."

"But he has to get at least an hour of volunteer

points, or he won't pass the semester." She pulled her friend closer. "We're not moving until we find out what team darling Darling is on."

"Or, better yet, get him on ours," Mira added in a giddy whisper.

Agnes caught sight of the teenage boy ambling over, stopping every few steps while his leashed dog sniffed the grass. Of course they'd be all over Mr. Swoony. And if he didn't have a partner...

"Move along, girls. There's a line forming," Agnes said, gesturing for them to step away.

Mira narrowed her eyes at Agnes. "There's no line. And we're not ready to leave yet."

Oh, really? She shot a sideways look at Finnie, who already had both her brows raised at the insolence. Giving a fake smile of her own, Agnes sneakily reached down without taking her eyes off them and unclipped Gala's leash.

Instantly, the little dog did what Agnes knew she would, taking off in the direction of her beloved Pru.

"Oh dear," Agnes said, pretending to be shocked.

"Your dog got away," the one named Mira said coolly.

"Go get him!" Finnie ordered with a rare edge in her voice. "Girls! What's wrong with you? Help an old lady out."

Agnes let the "old" comment pass as the two started—rather slowly—after the dog. "Gala won't get far," she told Finnie.

"Neither will those nasty creatures," Finnie added, then her smile brightened as a certain young man reached the table. "What a glorious greyhound, lad. What's his name?"

His eyes widened, as if he hadn't been expecting the greeting, and Agnes saw they were as dark and dreamy as the eyes of the Greek man she'd married.

"Uh, it's Tor," he said.

"And what team are you on, then?" Finnie beamed at him.

"Um…" He shook his head, making a lock of dark hair brush his forehead.

Oh yes, this young man was a looker.

"I'm not going to be on that list," he said. "I don't have a team."

Without a second's hesitation, Agnes grabbed the team list. "I know just the teammate for you."

"I don't need a team," he said, one hand on his dog's head. "Just a list of those…rack things."

Behind him, Agnes could see that the girls had caught Gala and were trying to get her back to the table. She'd have to move fast.

"Everyone needs a team, young man. RACKing cannot be done alone if Bitter Bark High is going to win this." She reached her hand, palm up, out to Finnie. "Glasses, please, so I can get this nice young man on the *perfect* team."

She braced for a surly look from him, the same one she'd just gotten from the girls. But he gave her the slightest hint of a smile, which made those dark eyes just a little darker and dreamier. Oh yes. Pru would thank her for this.

"Thanks, but I have Tor."

Just then, Pyggie stepped out from under the table to inspect Tor, startling the bigger dog. Tor rose up with a bark, snapping his jaws and snagging the glasses Finnie was holding out to Agnes. Shocked, the boy dropped the leash to try to free the glasses from Tor's teeth, but the dog took off with his prize, tearing toward the sleigh.

"Hey, Tor, no!" the boy shouted, suddenly in hot pursuit of a dark brown head and a snow-white body that had obviously been trained to do one thing very well—*run*. "Tor! Stop!"

"Oh my word," Finnie exclaimed. "My glasses!"

"Quick, let's get him on the list with Pru," Agnes said, grabbing a pen.

"Pru's coming with us to the mall."

"Lucas Darling," Agnes said, frantic to accomplish her goal. "On a team with Pru."

Finnie frowned and shook her head. "No, Agnes! He's a wee bit…unknown. And maybe best kept that way."

"Finola Kilcannon," Agnes chided. "Did you hear Pru's voice when she told us she'd been ditched by her friends? Did you see her staring at Hot Stuff? Do you not want Pru to have *some* fun on Christmas Eve? For heaven's sake, are we not the Dogmothers? This is child's play for us after the matches we've made."

It was easy to see the doubt in Finnie's eyes, especially without her glasses. "I don't think that's the kind of lad I'd choose for our sweet Pru."

"How do you know?"

"Just by the looks of him, I think—"

"Finnie! Did you take my judgy pills instead of your calcium this morning?"

She didn't laugh, but squinted as the boy came back, the leash in one hand—Tor attached—the glasses in the other. What was left of the glasses, that was.

"Man, I'm really…" He glanced at the mangled specs. "Wow. Sorry."

He held the glasses out. One of the nose pads was askew, and both arms were badly bent. "Geez," he breathed. "Tor, that was really bad. Even for you."

The greyhound came around the table and dropped his head in front of Agnes with that look of a dog who knows he's about to be disciplined.

But the boy crouched down and put his arm around the dog's long, narrow neck and head. "No worries, my dude. I know you're sorry. It's okay." His words were soft, whispered into Tor's ear with the same warmth and directness Agnes had seen from so many kids in Finnie's family, their love of dogs simply infectious. "He gets a little rambunctious," he said to Agnes and Finnie. "Raised as a racer, and they weren't…good to him. Anything shiny or small gets him going because they used shiny lures to train him."

His tenderness and rationalizations nearly cracked the heart that Agnes liked to deny she had. She turned to Finnie, pleased to see her gaze had warmed a bit as she observed him.

"'Tis all right, lad," Finnie said. "I have another pair at home."

He looked up at her with shockingly intense eyes, a shadow of pain and surprise and maybe distrust in them, as if he, too, expected discipline. "I can repay you. I don't know how, but—"

"I know how," Agnes said. "You are officially part of our team. You and Tor and…" She smiled at Finnie. "The Dogmothers."

"The Dogmothers?" His lips hitched in a half smile.

"Hi, Lucas!" The dynamic duo returned, Mira pulling Gala by the collar.

"Hey." He scowled at her. "Don't drag a dog like that."

Instantly, she let go of the collar, and Gala scampered back to Agnes, who scooped up the little doxie and stroked her head lovingly. "Good girl, Gala. Sorry you had to take one for the team."

"What team is she on?" Lucas asked Agnes. "'Cause that's a cute dog."

"Believe it or not, she's on our team." Agnes smiled at him.

"The Dogmothers?" he asked with a glint of humor in his eyes. "Cool. You want me to try and straighten those glasses?" He gave Gala's head a quick rub and looked at Agnes one more time.

Agnes turned to Finnie, who fiddled with the frames, then slid them on so that they sat utterly lopsided on her sweet face. "I can see, so I guess it's not so bad."

When he took a few steps away with Tor, Agnes leaned close to Finnie. "And he can join us?"

She nodded. "Aye."

"Now there's the Finnie I know and love," Agnes said.

"Well, he loves his dog, so how bad can he be?"

"Exactly."

And if she could just persuade her best friend to see the good in Aldo Fiore later today, it would be an excellent Christmas Eve for everyone. Especially sweet Prudence, who would certainly thank Agnes for this little Christmas gift.

Chapter Three

B y the time Pru finished answering the last of the
questions, helping some people figure out the
RACK IT UP app, and talking to Emma and
Charlotte—*and* Mason and Dylan, the boyfriends who
ranked higher on the food chain than Pru—it was
getting a little late.

She hurried across the square where Gramma
Finnie and Yiayia were still at the table, looking as if
they were eager to go. Of course, Yiayia wanted to get
to the Santa-stalking mission ASAP.

"Hey, guys, sorry that took so long," Pru called as
she got closer. "But we'll make it to..." The word
caught in her throat as Lucas Darling ambled closer,
his ebony gaze pinned on her. "Vestal..." She
couldn't remember the rest.

She'd never actually made eye contact with this
guy before, never really had the chance to look right
into the darkest, most penetrating gaze she could
remember. The effect was...dizzying.

"Do you need a RACK list?" she managed to ask.
"The teams are set, but you could—"

"I'm on your team."

She just stared at him, trying to swallow as the impossibility of what he'd just said settled on her chest. The one where her heart was suddenly beating double time. "Excuse me?"

"Unless Tor isn't welcome." He tugged the dog leash and made the greyhound prance a little closer. "Or I'm not."

She blinked at him, then turned to the grannies, doing a double take at the crooked frames on Gramma Finnie's face. "What happened to your glasses?"

"'Tis a minor setback," she said brightly, trying to straighten the glasses, but succeeding only in making them sit even more cockeyed on her tiny face. "I can see fine."

She shifted her gaze to Yiayia, who suddenly seemed wildly preoccupied with straightening the lists and refusing to make eye contact.

"It was my dog," Lucas said, taking a step closer. "Tor snagged her glasses and ran."

"Snagged…off her face?"

"Of course not," Gramma Finnie assured her. "Tor's a good dog. He's just…impulsive."

And Gramma was defending this?

"Tor." Pru looked at the greyhound, who was, she had to admit, almost as stunning a creature as his owner. Big, shiny, and athletic, with gorgeous brown eyes. "Short for Tornado?" she guessed, fighting a smile as the dog tilted his head and practically begged to be loved.

"Toreador was his racing name," Lucas said. "And seriously, um, Pru, I'm happy to fly solo."

She gave in to that smile when he put *um* and *Pru* together and got Umproo, the nickname her father had called her since the evening they met in a vet office.

And if she'd learned anything from Trace Bancroft, it was not to judge a book by its cover or a guy by his reputation.

And really, was this the *worst* thing to ever happen to her?

"No need to fly solo," she said. "Although, brace yourself with these two..." She tipped her head toward the grannies. "You may never be the same after a day with them."

"You don't have to come with us," Yiayia said quickly. "The two of you can just..." She made her fingers walk off. "Take off and randomly be...kind. We'll be fine on our little mission to the mall. You'll have much more fun alone."

Alone? Oh. Realization dawned as she eyed one little granny and then the other. The matchmakers never took a day off, did they?

Apparently not.

"I'm going with you, and that is final." God only knew what trouble they'd get into without her. And Pru didn't want to think about what kind of trouble she'd get into with...the Darling boy.

"Oh, lassie, we're grown women who can handle ourselves."

"Stalking a mobster dressed as Santa?" she asked under her breath so Lucas couldn't hear.

"He's not a—"

Pru silenced Yiayia with the sweep of her hand. "I'm going with you, and you..." She turned to Lucas, who was studying her again, his square jaw set with a surprising amount of determination, and...were those some whiskers on his hollowed cheeks? Jeez. "You don't have to do this," she finished.

"I want to."

Good God, was he serious? Maybe he didn't fully understand.

"You want to get in the car—*a Buick, mind you*—with my great-grandmothers and two dogs and drive half an hour to the county's monster mall—*on Christmas Eve*—where you will be expected to walk around and do nice things for perfect strangers *and take pictures of it?*" She spoke a little slowly because maybe he was nothing more than a gorgeous empty head with long, thick, finger-tempting black hair.

"Three dogs. 'Cause Tor goes where I go." He smiled, showing off a set of dimples that put the eyes and hair and jaw to shame. "And I'm pretty sure this whole state is dog-friendly, including a mall."

Seriously? All day with this...this *hotness?* How could she possibly RACK UP POINTS with a thousand butterflies suddenly airborne in her stomach and her knees threatening to buckle?

"How did this even happen?" she asked on a bewildered sigh.

"I need community service hours for this semester, and I want to—"

"You can just walk around Bitter Bark and give kids dog stickers," she said. "My mom's a vet, so I have some in my bag. And I have candy canes."

"I want to go," he finished.

She stared at him for a second, trying to decide if there could possibly be something genuine under all that windblown long hair and butter-soft leather jacket.

"Okay," she finally said, since a good general always knew when to back down. "Let's go to Vestal Village Mall." She slid a look to Gramma Finnie.

"Won't be the first time we did something crazy on Christmas Eve."

"And it won't be the last," Finnie said, turning to Yiayia. "Unless we end up swimming with the fishes."

"What?" Lucas asked.

"Nothing," Pru said, adding a warning look to the grannies.

A few minutes later, they were piled into Yiayia's Buick Regal. And even that boat was barely big enough for three dogs—one fat, one needy, and one stretched out across the back seat with his head on Lucas's lap and his back paws on Pru's—plus two octogenarians, one almost six-foot-tall future Zac Efron, and Pru.

Doing her part to save space, Pru pressed against the car door in case she had to jump out onto the highway at any second, or at least press her warm cheek to the cool glass.

How in the world had this day gone from a fun time running around Bitter Bark with Emma and Charlotte to...Darling and the Dogmothers?

"So, I understand you're new in town, lad." From the front passenger seat, Gramma Finnie turned a bit to direct her question to the boy sitting directly behind her. "Pru says you're from California."

Oh sure, Gramma. Let him know I talked about him. That's just great.

"Yeah, LA." He looked down at the dog on his lap, stroking his massive head with a hand that looked big and strong and—

Stop staring at his hands, Pru.

"What brings you here?" Yiayia asked.

"Just…family stuff."

"Did your parents move, too?" Yiayia pressed. "And did you get this dog here or there? Do you like Bitter Bark? It's probably so different from Los Angeles. How long are you staying?"

He gave a soft laugh at the barrage of questions, shooting a look at Pru, who just lifted a shoulder. "Hey, you ride with the grannies, you pay the price."

"It's okay," he said. "Grandmas are my comfort zone."

She frowned a little, totally not expecting that.

"I'm living with my aunt and uncle," he said to the ladies in the front.

So *that* much of the rumor mill was true.

"I'm here until…" He let out a breath. "For a while. And yeah, Bitter Bark's different, but it's kind of like a movie set, you know."

Movie set? Maybe he did have Hollywood connections.

He slid a look at Pru that made those butterflies rise up for the second spin around her belly. "What else did she ask?" he mouthed.

"The dog."

"Oh yeah. Tor is…" He shook his head. "A really good, uh, friend of mine adopted him, and then she…" His voice trailed off.

She. A girlfriend in LA, of course.

"She had to give him up," he finished with just enough angst in his voice that Pru suddenly had it all figured out. He'd met his match, some crazy-hot blond actress and Instagram star, no doubt. He fell hard for her, and her dog, then she got a part in a movie and broke his heart by leaving and sticking him

27

with her dog. Sure, she promised to come back and get him, but would she?

"But he's been a good bud," he added, then laughed, flashing the dimples that really ought to be illegal. "Well, not *good*. Tor is a little bit, um, undisciplined. He can run, but he doesn't quite have the whole rule thing figured out."

"Well, you have landed in a family of dog trainers, lad," Gramma Finnie said.

Gramma! Pru tried not to choke. He hadn't exactly *landed in the family*.

"Really?" Lucas sat up a little. "Tor could probably use some of that."

"My son runs the largest canine training and rescue center in the state," she said proudly.

"Your dad?" he asked Pru.

"Actually, my grandfather owns Waterford Farm, but my dad's one of the trainers of therapy dogs. And my uncles are all some of the best trainers around. And my mom's a vet."

"Get out." He looked skyward. "Man, you must think Tor is a nightmare."

"Tor's sweet," Pru said, patting the dog's hindquarters and adjusting the two long, long legs on her thighs. "He certainly isn't shy."

"That makes one of us," Lucas said with a soft, self-deprecating laugh.

He was shy? She filed that away for something to mull over later. No doubt she'd be doing a lot of mulling after today. She might never be able to answer another question in English lit for the rest of the year, she'd be so busy *mulling* over the boy who sat in the back row next to the pencil sharpener.

She might just spend the whole class…sharpening her pencils instead of her lit skills.

"My dad says it's never the dog's fault, it's the trainer's."

He notched one brow at the little dig. "I must be a wreck, then, because Tor?" He pushed his ears down. "Is bad to the bone."

She had to laugh, something about him reminding her again of that day when she met Dad and had no idea he was her father, just an ex-con with scary tattoos and an ailing dog. And look how much she loved…

Oh God. *Control the crush, Prudence. Control the crush.*

She shifted in her seat, gave him a cool smile, and looked out the window. She couldn't like this boy. Sure, he was eye candy, and all the girls giggled about him when he showed up at school, but she was Prudence Anne Kilcannon Bancroft, number one in her class, bound for Chapel Hill or maybe Duke, based on her PSATs. She didn't date guys like Lucas Darling.

And Lucas Darling sure as heck didn't date girls like Pru.

Who didn't date anyone…yet. Not a single boy had ever asked her out, and she was sixteen. Maybe it was her reputation as a general—some boys didn't like girls who were leaders. Or maybe it was all her uncles and her dad with tattoos and his own questionable past. Or maybe she just wasn't pretty or flirtatious or whatever it was boys wanted.

She hadn't figured it out yet. But she certainly didn't want to start her boy journey with Lucas Darling. Talk about setting herself up for failure.

"Right, Pru?"

She blinked at Yiayia's question, lost. "Uh, yeah, sure."

"Really?" Lucas seemed a little surprised by whatever she'd just agreed to. "You'd do that?"

Oh God, *what*?

"Because I could really use some help training Tor, so if you know some tricks..."

She'd agreed to help him train the dog? "Oh, I don't know anything that you couldn't find on YouTube, I'm sure."

She could feel Yiayia's glare, delivered through the rearview mirror directly at Pru. Of course, she could only imagine the words Yiayia was trying not to say. *Hey, the Dogmothers made you a match, missy. Don't blow it.* She looked away, glancing instead at the boy next to her, not expecting to see a little flash of disappointment at her response.

Did he *want* her to help him train Tor? Or...had her dismissive comment actually hurt his feelings? Would a guy that hot even *have* feelings?

She cleared her throat and tried to think about dog training. No easy feat in the face of that...face. "It's always good to train with a toy he loves," she finally said. "Does he like toys?"

"For breakfast. Then what's left of them goes in the trash." He petted the dog again. "Since they train racing dogs by having them chase a lure, he gets kind of overly focused on things. Like..." He jutted his chin toward Gramma Finnie. "Glasses. And pens. And phones—I don't have one right now because he ate it."

"You don't have a phone?"

"My aunt has to sign for me to get one, and she's out of town for a few days."

"On Christmas Eve?" Yiayia and Gramma Finnie asked the question in perfect, shocked unison.

"They had plans," he said vaguely, looking a little uncomfortable. "It's fine."

"Christmas alone is never fine," Gramma Finnie said.

Oh boy. She was about to issue an invitation to Christmas Eve dinner at Waterford Farm. Pru could hear the words before they were formed in her little Irish head. *Oh, lad, ye must come to dinner...*

"You're in my English lit class," Pru said quickly, hoping to head off the invitation before it was issued.

"Yeah," he said. "And I can't believe old Thorgrim gave us homework over winter break."

"Just reading," she said. "That's not work. Although, I guess you..."

He tipped his head. "Contrary to rumors, I can read. And not just comic books and video game screens."

A splash of shame heated her cheeks, making her swallow and hold his gaze long enough to at least try to let him know she was sorry. "So, did you pick *Jekyll and Hyde* or *Sense and Sensibility?*" *Gah, dumb question, Pru.* Not one guy in the class would read Jane Austen.

"I already read *Sense and Sensibility*," he said, making her draw back in surprise. "In fact, I've already read everything on the list. Thorgrim said I could pick something else."

Well, color her...impressed. "California schools must be ahead of North Carolina."

He lifted a shoulder. "Or I might just read for fun."

"Jane Austen?" she asked, unable to keep that one inside.

"My, um, friend liked Austen."

Oh, the movie star girlfriend who broke his heart. Wow, he'd read Jane Austen for her? That was... really stinking attractive.

"Okay, it looks like we're at the mall," Gramma Finnie announced as they stared at a line of red brake lights about a mile long after they got off the highway.

"And we might have parked in Bitter Bark and gotten inside faster." Yiayia let out an exasperated sigh.

"I told you this place would be packed." Pru checked her phone. Would they have enough time to rack up RACK points?

"While you're on your phone, Pru," Yiayia said, "can you check the mall's website? Maybe they have information about the Santa schedule."

"Sure, although I'm sure Santa's already at work," she said, tapping the screen. "Just let me check the RACK IT UP app real quick."

"They came to see Santa?" Lucas asked Pru in a whisper, understandably confused.

No, they came to spy on a mobster who Yiayia is considering dating. "He's...a friend of theirs."

Another look from Yiayia. Pru flashed one right back. Did she really want to be *that* honest with a complete stranger?

"I think he mentioned that he may only do the morning shift," Yiayia said, stress tightening her voice.

"Then he has to go put a hit on his bookie," Gramma added softly.

Lucas's eyes widened. "What?"

Pru waved off the question with a nervous laugh. "Inside joke."

"This is going to take hours." Yiayia tapped the steering wheel with impatience. "I'm going to *miss* him."

Lucas shifted in his seat, no doubt starting to get the idea these ladies were cray-cray. "Take this right," he said.

"That's the wrong direction," Pru told him. "The mall's over there."

"Take the right," he repeated.

"Says the guy from California."

He just smiled. "The same guy who was here a week ago with his aunt who knows a back way into the Macy's parking lot."

Yiayia whipped out of the traffic. "I'm game," she said.

In a moment, they found a side street, Lucas gave more directions, and before long, Yiayia parked the Buick within sight of the Macy's entrance.

"You, my son, are a genius!" she exclaimed as she threw the car into park. "I'm so glad we brought you."

"At least someone is," he murmured, the soft-spoken zinger hitting Pru right in the gut.

She looked up from her phone, expecting that dark gaze to be nothing less than disgusted with her. But there was just enough of a tease and a challenge in his eyes that her heart flipped around and went tumbling down into the butterfly pit.

Then he winked...and she was toast.

Chapter Four

Agnes checked her reflection in the glass doors as the crew marched into Macy's at the massive two-story Vestal Village Mall. She smoothed a stray black hair and checked her lipstick, feeling confident and attractive enough to catch the eye of Aldo Fiore.

"Don't worry, Agnes, you look gorgeous," Finnie whispered as they stepped into the warm air of the department store.

"Hardly."

Finnie smiled. "I like when you are humble," she said. "It's one of your best looks."

Agnes smiled, always appreciating Finnie's unending attempts to help Agnes's self-improvement efforts. Finnie was one of the few people who knew that a little more than two years ago, a heart attack had had Agnes literally knocking on heaven's door, only to be sent back with some vague instructions to "do better." From that day on, Agnes Santorini had set about to change herself, inside and out.

It had been relatively easy to lose weight, have a few injections, dye her hair, and shave a few years off of Agnes Santorini. She'd never felt healthier or stronger. But, oh, the inner changes had been a little more challenging.

It hadn't been easy to soften a sharp tongue or dial back her natural sarcasm or even reserve judgment after a lifetime of passing it on everyone and everything. But each year, especially since she'd forged a friendship and family connection with sweet Finnie and her loving clan, Agnes had gotten closer to what she thought was a *changed* life.

And now, for the first time in years, she longed for another change, this one with a man. She had no desire to get married again, or even fall in love, nothing so permanent or serious. But all the family matchmaking she and Finnie had been doing had awakened something Agnes had thought had gone to sleep for good.

Now, she sometimes opened her eyes in the middle of the night and ached for the feel of her dear Nik by her side. She remembered the thrill of having his warm lips on hers and the deep comfort of threading her fingers through his. She liked the smell of a freshly showered man, the power of a deep voice, and the sense of balance in her life when it included a loving man.

She'd had fun this past fall with old Max Hewitt, plotting the romance between Finnie's grandson Declan and Max's granddaughter Evie. She liked Max, as a friend and card player. And he certainly held his own in the matchmaking game. But she didn't feel a zing with Max, and for all his flirting, he was truly a one-woman man, biding his time until he could join his beloved Penny in heaven.

But the mild flirtation had driven Agnes to try

something all new—a dating website exclusively for older people.

Her very first "match" had been a silver fox named Aldo. From his first text, he'd made her smile with a quick wit and genuine warmth. After a week of banter and text exchanges, he'd told her his full name and asked if she'd meet him for lunch sometime between Christmas and New Year's.

When she'd told Finnie, her best friend had flipped her Irish lid and announced Aldo Fiore was some kind of Mafia don hiding out in Sweetheart Springs.

Which had to be hogwash...Agnes hoped.

"How are they doing back there?" Finnie turned to look at Pru and Lucas walking behind them as the group made their way down the wide tiled floor between dresses nobody should be caught dead in and some ghastly seasonal sweaters already on sale.

Agnes glanced at the teenagers, who were alternately talking and checking each other out when they thought the other one didn't notice. "Love is in the air. Can't you see that?"

Gramma tried to straighten her glasses. "I can't see too much of anything, truth be told. But aye, 'tis a bit more fun for a—*oh*!"

All of a sudden, Tor launched between Finnie and Agnes, nearly tripping over the doxies, his long, lean body slicing through everything in its path as he tore toward a jewelry counter.

"Whoa! Tor!" Despite his size, Lucas was yanked by the leash, barely able to stop the dog as he tried to pounce on a stack of gold earrings, his teeth just missing a sparkling ornament decorating the display. "Easy, boy!"

The tower of jewelry tipped one way, then the other, but Pru managed to grab the table and save the whole thing from toppling over. Lucas put both arms around Tor and somehow held him back from taking a second swipe.

"Yikes." Pru gave a quick laugh in the face of Agnes's and Finnie's shocked looks. "Disaster averted."

"Barely," Agnes said, tugging her own leashes to calm Pyggie and Gala, who barked noisily at the disruption. "Are you prepared to pay for anything he destroys?"

The boy looked down, as chastised as the dog. "He's, um, never been in a place like this before."

Once again, the contrition in his voice matched the big sad eyes of the dog, and Agnes's heart shifted, proving it really wasn't made of stone anymore.

"Well, be careful," she said, just as the dog dropped to the ground in a heap. "Oh! Is he okay?"

"This is kind of what he does," Lucas said. "He was raised as a sprinter, so he gets these bursts of energy and gets really focused on something, then he gets so exhausted, he has to rest. It's a greyhound thing."

"Sounds like a senior thing," Agnes said with a sly smile, making them laugh.

"Just keep a hold of him, lad," Finnie warned as a group of people tried to get by them all. "'Tis a busy day and a crowded place."

He nodded. "Yes, ma'am. He'll be fine."

Agnes looked around as the crowd cleared, spotting the entrance to the mall just past the makeup counters. "All righty, then, we'll meet you two back here in, what, two hours?"

Pru looked slightly horrified at the suggestion. "Oh, no, Yiayia. We don't want to be….We'll go with you guys," she said.

"Pru, that's not necessary," Agnes said. "The last thing I want to do is draw Aldo's attention to us, and *this* group?" Her gaze shifted to the animal the size of a reindeer literally *snoring* on the floor of Macy's. "Is an attention magnet."

"You'll never know we're there," Pru assured her, shifting a heavy backpack on her shoulder. "I've got all the RACK materials in this bag, and we'll just follow you and quietly perform our Random Acts of Christmas Kindness on the way. Do you have your list?" she asked Lucas.

He gave her a look like he'd never heard of a list.

"Hang on." Pru put her bag down and knelt next to it, and the very act shot a punch of irritation through Agnes.

"We do *not* have all day," she said, strident enough to get one of those warning looks from Finnie. But this time, a little sharpness was called for. "Prudence, you have a partner. He's very nice. You do not need to keep us from our mission in order to accomplish yours."

"Just give me a second to find his list…" She whipped out a pack of papers, then another, setting them on the floor. "I made a special one for my team. It's in here somewhere."

Agnes sighed, shifting from one foot to the other, knowing she was being petulant, but…*Aldo*. What if his Santa shift ended at noon? "Time's a-wastin', Prudence," she said.

"Let me help you," Lucas said, crouching down to get next to her.

Pru glanced at him, a little color rising in her cheeks. "Oh, that's…" Their hands bumped as they both reached for some papers, making both of them jerk back, and Agnes could have sworn the lights flickered from the bolt of electricity in the room.

"Is this it?" Lucas asked, holding out a brightly colored piece of paper with a glittery red border Agnes recognized as the stationery Pru's mother used for her holiday letters. He shook it a little, raining red sparkles on the ground. "Whoa. The glitter bomb has exploded."

Pru gave a self-conscious laugh. "What can I say? I like Christmas."

He waved the paper, and more red flakes danced through the air like fairy dust around both of them.

Agnes slid a look at Finnie, who was watching them, fighting a smile.

"Let's go," Agnes mouthed, giving her a nudge toward the door. "They're *fine*."

"So fine," Finnie agreed, but hesitated long enough for the big dog to sit up and snap at the sparkly paper, digging his teeth right into it, then flipping his head from side to side like he had a glittery mouse in his jaws instead of Pru's paper.

"Oh no!" Pru cried.

"Tor!" Lucas reached for the paper, tearing it out of his mouth, but the dog held tight to his half, chewing it like the sparkles were made of bacon.

"Good heavens!" Finnie exclaimed. "He does need some training."

The boy's shoulders fell. "I know, I'm really…" He swallowed, as if *sorry* wouldn't cut it.

"That was my only list," Pru said softly.

Tor stared at her, chewing.

"We can save this," Lucas assured her, spreading the half page on the floor with one hand and sticking his finger in Tor's mouth to try to get the other half out. Instantly, Pyggie waddled over with his *I'll have what that dog's having* face.

"No, no," Lucas and Pru said in unison, while Agnes tugged his leash. Immediately, Gala barked in horror, sensing the chaos in the air.

Pru let out a sigh like she sensed it, too. "Go on, Yiayia," she finally said. "Gala's upset. We'll meet you at Santa's Workshop in a little bit. This could take a while."

She nodded her thanks and gave Finnie another nudge. "Let's go, Finn."

Once again, Finnie hesitated, looking down at Pru. "Call me if you need anything, lass."

"You call me," Pru said. "And don't have fun without me, Dogmothers!"

With a quick wave, Finnie turned and hustled along with Agnes.

"Sweet Saint Patrick there's a little chemistry between those two."

Agnes grinned. "We're getting really good at this matchmaking."

"But ye see she's torn and wants to be with us." Finnie sighed. "My dear Prudence, on the precipice of womanhood, but still a wee lass."

"She's not wee. She's sixteen and could use a little male attention," Agnes replied, tugging Finnie into the bustling mall with Gala and Pyggie leading them on. "And so could I, so move it, Finola Kilcannon."

Finnie clucked as they threaded their way through

the throngs of shoppers, past a group of carolers belting out *Joy to the World*, and spent some time detained by a ten-car train on its way to Santa's Workshop outside the food court. The only time they voluntarily slowed was to check out the contained, AstroTurfed play area for dogs, which had plenty of pups running around.

"Maybe that rambunctious dog could run off some of his energy in here," Finnie mused.

"Except he'd jump the fence, eat the decorations, and scare the poor little ones half to death."

Finnie laughed. "The boy loves him, though."

"I can see that," Agnes agreed.

"I always say you can tell a lot about a man by how he treats his dog."

"I thought you always say it's how he treats his kids." Agnes stood on her toes to see over the crowd, spotting the Santa's Workshop sign and a massive tree draped in gold and red. "There he is! Santa!"

A woman walking by shot her a surprised and somewhat disgusted look.

"What's her problem?" Agnes muttered.

"You're never too old for Santa!" Finnie called out as the woman walked away.

Agnes squeezed her friend's arm. "God, I love you, Finnie."

In front of them, Gala pranced a little, always in tune with a rise in excitement. She must have known Agnes's heart was pounding as they got closer.

"He's over there, on the other side," Finnie said. "Facing the food court. Let's get ourselves situated at a table, and we can watch him in action."

"Good plan, but can we just walk by first? Not too

close, although I doubt he'd recognize me from that picture."

"The one taken in 1980?" Finnie teased.

Agnes laughed lightly, knowing she sounded a little like those teenage girls giddy over Lucas, but she didn't care. Crushes knew no age. "Let's cruise by him, real nonchalant," Agnes said. "I want to get a good look and be sure it's him under the beard and fat suit."

"Off we go, lassie."

And she did feel like a lassie, for the first time in years. Hooking arms and letting the dachshunds part the crowd for them, they made their way around the giant tree surrounded by huge red boxes and bright gold ribbons.

As they came around to the food court side, she got her first real look at him.

Well, as good as it could be considering he was covered in a fur-trimmed red suit and wore a white beard. But she could see those dark eyes and his straight Roman nose. He was tall, too, probably six feet, with broad enough shoulders, considering he was eighty.

Just as they got a little closer, he *ho, ho, ho'd* a little boy off his lap, handing him over to his mother, an attractive woman in her thirties. Santa said something that made the woman throw her head back with a hearty laugh.

"See? He's funny," Agnes said, tamping down a little bolt of unexpected jealousy when the woman said something that made Santa laugh, too.

"Can we get a little closer?" Finnie asked, adjusting her crooked glasses. "I can't quite see him."

"You can. I don't want to draw his attention."

"Stay on the other side of me," Finnie said.

Swept up in the moment, Agnes agreed, letting Finnie lead them to the roped off area, nestling up to a few parents taking pictures. They were close enough for Agnes to see the sparkle in Aldo's eyes that wasn't an act for the kids.

"Better get a Ferrari under the tree," he said to the woman. "Fortunately, I think he means a toy remote-control Ferrari, or you'd be out a few hundred grand."

The woman smiled. "That'd be a problem since I'm a single mother."

"You are?" He inched closer. "Are you in the market for a husband?"

What?

Finnie gasped softly, inching back, proving that Agnes had heard that correctly. Finnie instantly turned away. "Let's get out of here, Agnes," she whispered harshly.

But Agnes didn't move, mesmerized by what was unfolding in front of her and vaguely aware that Finnie was walking away. Agnes knew she should follow, but something stopped her. In fact, something drove her closer to listen to the exchange.

"Of course I am," the woman said. "But there are very few men who want to take on a wife and a child."

"Then leave your number and—"

Next to her, a child squealed, making it impossible to hear the rest of what he said.

Really, Aldo? Her faith in mankind, always on shaky ground, tumbled around a little in her chest.

"I'm only interested in a man in his thirties, responsible, and likes to cook," the woman said as the kid beside Yiayia sucked in air between screams.

As Aldo replied, Gala was barking at the screamer, the mall train whistle blew, and the kid hit high C louder than the carolers crooning *It Came Upon a Midnight Clear.*

Then the young mother gave a business card to Aldo, who grinned and tucked it in his pocket.

Was he a cad? A player? A flirtatious Lothario? God knew Agnes already had had one of those in her life, so many years ago, before Nik saved her. That kind of man was the last thing she'd ever want again.

But the woman had been clear in her list of must-haves and still had given him her number, so…what had he said to her? He certainly didn't meet the "in his thirties" criteria.

On a sigh, Agnes went to hunt for Finnie. Part of her wanted to run and forget this whole crazy thing. But part of her knew there was still much to learn about Aldo Fiore. And she wasn't quite ready to write him off.

Chapter Five

Of all the things Pru had thought might happen today, discovering that Lucas Darling wasn't a scary, intimidating, unapproachable hottie with a *baditude* was not anything she'd have put on her to-do list when she'd rolled out of bed.

Shockingly, he was kind of...darling. Just like his dog, who wasn't bad, not really. He was kind of darling, too. Shy and understated, but so impressive that people couldn't look away or resist stopping to pet him.

No surprise, a good many of those "people" were female, under eighteen, and flipped their hair when they talked in sentences that sounded like questions even when they weren't. But to his credit, Lucas didn't flirt back and was super protective of Tor. Having been raised in a big family that built its whole business around dogs, Pru gave him props for that.

And for his valiant effort to save her glitter-covered list of the most creative ideas for Random Acts of Christmas Kindness.

"Can you read any of it?" he asked as Pru studied what was left on the list she'd prepared for her original teammates.

"Some," she said, squinting at the list. "We were going to start our day by going into my aunt's dog treat store, buy a bunch of treats, and hand them out in Bushrod Square. But now we're here, so…"

"I know there's a pet store here, and they have puppies in kennels. We could give them treats."

"They probably won't let you. Plus." She made a face. "Who would buy their dog from a mall when there are a million rescues out there?"

"Mall dogs need homes, too, Pru," he said with a little tease in his eyes. Actually, that spark of humor was always there, she'd noticed. Not at school, but here he seemed a lot less daunting.

"I take it Tor is a rescue."

He nodded, reaching down to pet the dog who, for once, strode along between them without darting, dashing, or getting distracted. "From Florida."

"Florida? How did you get him in California?"

"From…a friend."

Oh, right, the ex-girlfriend. She recognized the vagueness in his tone every time he talked about her. "How did your friend get him in Florida?"

"She…" He swallowed, visibly tense. "She had to go there for a family thing and ended up coming back with Tor." A smile threatened as though the memory touched him. "Then…" He took a slow breath and let it out like whatever was to follow caused him genuine agony.

"She had to give him up," Pru helped when he didn't seem like he could even finish the sentence.

46

"Yeah." He turned away, looking hard at a Justice store as if bedazzled sweaters for preteens interested him. So Pru went digging for another topic.

"So, some Christmas Eve, huh?" she asked.

He shrugged, still looking away. "It's fine."

"My great-grannies are nuts, though."

"I like them." He turned to her now, that humor back. "I'm still confused, though. Are they both related to you?"

"Gramma Finnie is my mother's grandmother. And she practically raised me, right along with my mother and Grannie Annie, who's passed."

"Finnie's the one with the accent."

"She's from Ireland."

"She's a cool lady."

The compliment warmed her. "She's the best. She writes a hilarious little blog all about dogs and our family business and the town, and she embroiders pillows. Oh, and she can drink a truck driver under the table."

"Really?" He snorted a laugh. "Sounds about right. And the other grandma?"

"Okay, I'll explain it, but it's complicated."

He pinned that insane gaze on her, and suddenly Pru felt like she could recite the entire enormous three-branch family tree and he'd care. Was that possible? Bad boy Lucas Darling?

Who'da thunk it?

"My grandfather was a widower, and he got remarried to a woman who used to be Yiayia's daughter-in-law."

He frowned. "Oookay."

"Except that this woman's oldest son is also my

grandfather's son, because they used to date, and she got pregnant and..." She laughed at his incredulous face. "I'm losing you."

"Kinda, but I don't mind listening." He angled his head so one of his locks of dark hair slipped over his forehead and kissed a brow.

Kissed? What the heck was wrong with her?

"Well, short version is it's a huge family with a lot of add-ons," she said quickly. "I have, like, twenty aunts and uncles, half a dozen cousins, and they all have a million dogs. And one Greek great-grandmother who somehow fits right in."

"Sounds like fun."

Really? He thought that? "It is. Like tonight, everyone will be together for Christmas Eve dinner, and then we'll pile into Midnight Mass like the Irish and Greek armies. And...God, I need to shut up."

He gave a soft laugh that seemed like it came from deep inside his chest. "No, if I look stunned, it's just...wow. I don't have anything like that."

"Just your aunt here in Bitter Bark?" she guessed, somehow sensing that it would be very easy to make him turn away again. And she didn't want that. She could stare into those eyes for the entire day.

"Watch out," he said softly, snagging her jacket so she narrowly missed walking right into a cart of phone cases.

"Yikes," she muttered, looking ahead, busted for staring at him.

"Actually, I live with my aunt and my uncle. Well, they're kind of like Yiayia is to you."

"Tangentially related?" As soon as she used the SAT vocab word, she regretted it. Cute girls that he liked wouldn't say things like *tangentially*.

"Actually, no," he said, not blinking an eye at her word choice. "Not related at all, but very much like family."

"Oh, okay. Are they older?"

"Not really. Fifties."

"Then what did you mean when you said grandmas are your comfort zone?"

He gave her a quick look, something flashing in his eyes. Fear? Hurt? It was gone too quickly to decipher. "Long story," he said, turning again, this time to stare hard at Bath & Body Works soap displays.

"So, I wonder if I know your aunt and uncle," Pru said, finally getting comfortable with just talking to him. "Bitter Bark is a small town."

"They moved here a year ago."

"And you moved all the way from California to live with them?" She spun through all the possibilities and couldn't come up with anything but... "Did something happen to your parents?" she asked, trying to soften any horror and brace herself for something like *they died*.

"Yeah," he said on a laugh she totally didn't expect. "They had a kid they *really* didn't want sixteen years ago, split up, and kind of forgot I exist."

"Oh..." She didn't have any idea how to respond to that. "I'm...sorry."

"It's fine," he said. "They're just not, you know, my favorite people. But the Hernandezes are awesome." He eyed her, just enough to nudge the butterflies to life. "I know what you're thinking."

God, she hoped not. "You do?"

"They left me on Christmas, but it's cool. It was my choice not to go with them. I couldn't leave Tor in a kennel, and he sure as heck can't take another flight. The one from LA nearly killed him."

"Aww, poor baby." She patted the dog, then looked up at Lucas. "And that's not what I was thinking," she added.

"Your eyes are pretty much dead giveaways, Pru."

He was studying her eyes enough to know her thoughts? An unfamiliar heat curled through her, making her slow her step so she didn't trip or walk into another kiosk. "Well, if you must know—"

"I must," he said, making her laugh.

"I was thinking it was sad about your parents. My mom is my best friend, and my dad…" She closed her eyes for a second as she thought about Trace Bancroft. "He's the greatest."

"You're lucky, then."

"I know, but I only met him a few years ago," she admitted.

"So he's your stepdad?" he asked.

"No, he's my biological father."

He threw her a confused look. "And you just met him?"

She took a breath, almost ready to share her strange family story, but did she trust him? Did she even know him? After a moment, she shrugged and looked away, shifting her attention to Tor, who was pulling on the leash a little harder than he had been, his attention locked on a store just ahead.

"Oh, the pet store," Pru said, gesturing to The Animal House. "Should we attempt our first Random Act of Christmas Kindness in there?"

He looked a little dubious. "You think I should trust Tor…nado?"

She laughed at the nickname and touched the dog's long face, which didn't require her to bend much. His head practically reached Pru's chest. "Okay, doggo, here's the deal," she said. "You behave, and you get a treat."

His tail whipped back and forth as he looked up at her with sweet brown eyes. "You know what a treat is?" she asked.

"He knows what a pretty girl with a kind voice is."

Her heart did an unexpected flip at the compliment. "Well, do you think he'll follow the rules?"

"I'll hold him tight. What's your RACK plan?"

She had to smile, appreciating that he was into the school project enough to use the nickname. Flipping her backpack around, she unzipped a side pocket. "What you suggested. I'm going to buy a bunch of treats, and then we can take them over to that indoor dog park and give them to little kids to hand to the dogs. Sound kind?"

"Sounds like a recipe for a lawsuit if one of the dogs bites a kid."

She gasped. "I never thought of that! You have a better idea? 'Cause your dog ate all of mine."

Laughing, he looked into the store and thought for a moment. "You have money for this?"

"I have fifty dollars, but I don't want to spend it all in one store."

He nodded. "Let's give those dog stickers you mentioned to ten kids, each with a dollar to buy a dog treat, or do whatever they want with the money."

She thought about that and nodded. "Probably not

worth a truckload of points, but we'll make some kids happy. You want to stay out here with Tor and maybe take some pictures of me for the app?"

"I don't have a phone, remember?"

"Oh yeah. Well, you do the store stuff, then." She dug into the side pocket of her backpack and grabbed her wallet, taking out a ten.

"I can get it," he said, reaching into his back pocket.

"Next one. I've saved money just for this project." She also gave him the roll of stickers her mother gave to kids who came into her vet office with sick pets. "You'll just need to get ones from the cashier."

"Wow," he said under his breath. "Smart and generous."

She smiled, self-conscious as she handed him a ten-dollar bill. "Just…you know, resourceful."

"Take a compliment, Pru." He took the ten she handed him and playfully used it to brush under her chin. "I don't throw them out at just anybody." With a quick smile, he gave her the leash. "Do your dog training magic on Tor. He sure could use it."

As he walked away, she tugged the big dog closer, rubbing his head and steadying her breath. "So, Tornado," she whispered, staring at Lucas's broad shoulders in the leather jacket, his wayward long hair over the collar, his easy stride of confidence. "Your human is quite the surprise. A very pleasant surprise."

He fidgeted a little, his gaze as locked on Lucas as Pru's was.

She watched him enter the store and head toward the counter, slowing to look down at something that had a small group gathered around it.

"Puppies?" Pru guessed, letting the dog lead her a little bit closer. "We can peek, but don't go too close."

Lucas looked out toward her and pointed at whatever was on the floor. "You gotta see this," he mouthed.

Oh, and there went the butterflies, out of control at the very slightest connection she seemed to have with this kid. Only it wasn't *slight*. Or was she imagining that?

She was drawn to him like Tor was drawn to the pet store and what she imagined were some very enticing scents. "Easy, boy," she said, tightening her grip on the leash. "What is it?" she called to Lucas.

"Puppies."

As she'd thought. "Cute?"

He rolled his eyes like there was no way to describe *how* cute.

"Let's just take a peek, Tor." She took a few steps closer as Lucas went to the counter to get the change. "I love me some puppies."

As she got right at the entrance to the store, a few kids stepped away from the puppy bin, giving Pru a direct view into small cage full of five or six puppies of various breeds. A little yellow Lab, a tiny beagle, a Yorkie that could fit in her pocket, and, oh, was that a doxie?

"Look, Tor! A dachshund like your new friends, Pyggie and Gala." She was barely aware that she was inching closer until a woman in a red jacket with the store logo gestured to her.

"Dogs are welcome," she said. "And he is stunning."

"Isn't he?" she said with a surprising amount of pride. "This is Tor, a greyhound."

"Racer?" she asked.

"I...guess, yeah. He's not mine." She glanced at Lucas, watching him talk to the cashier and show him the stickers, no doubt explaining what they were doing, then at the six puppies cuddled behind a small wire fence.

"Well, bring him in and let him sniff," the lady said.

Sniff and...*destroy.*

But Tor seemed pretty chill, his laser focus on the puppies, staring hard at the one with long, floppy ears. "Oh, you like the basset, huh? Hound to hound, I guess."

He answered by pulling her closer to the small pen, and a few of the people around it automatically made space for the sizable dog. Tor lowered his head, sniffing, smashing his nose to the metal wires of the crate. Well, not exactly a crate, just one of those free-standing circle fences that her aunt Ella used at Bone Appetit to contain customers' dogs.

"You should probably be the one gated, Tor," she murmured, holding tight to his leash.

But he wasn't at all jumpy. In fact, he lowered himself to the ground and got nose to nose with the little chestnut and white basset baby, who seemed just as interested in him.

"Aww!"

"Look at those two!"

The people around them fussed, but Tor stayed riveted. Pru looked up and caught Lucas's eye as he fanned out the dollar bills in one hand and the roll of stickers in the other.

"Here I go," he said. "Take pictures so we get credit."

She fished out her phone, putting the leash under her sneaker so Tor wouldn't get away.

Then Lucas stepped toward a little girl about six years old and said to her mom, "I'm with a local high school doing Random Acts of Christmas Kindness. Can I give a sticker and a dollar to your daughter? She can use it to buy a treat for the dogs in the mall."

"Of course!" The woman beamed at him, clearly not immune to the charms of a bad boy with good looks.

As he offered them to the child, Pru took a picture. Lots of pictures. Couldn't have enough pictures of Lucas Darling, she decided, turning to follow him to the next child with the camera, keeping her foot on Tor's leash.

This time, she tapped the video icon and got the exchange with him explaining what they were doing.

Dang. He was good at this. He was adorable with the kids and charming with the moms, and every time he looked over at Pru and gave her a thumbs-up or a smile, her heart just…

Oh crap. She was crushing on the guy so hard. That was not supposed to happen.

Control the crush, Pru. Control the—

Tor suddenly stood, snapping her attention back to her first job—which was not to stare lovingly at Lucas Darling and admit she had a crush. Tor had zeroed in on the cashier now, who had pulled out a huge tray of dog treats for the kids to buy.

"Easy, boy." She bent over to get the leash, taking her foot off it for one nanosecond, but that was all it took for Tor to launch in the direction of the treats. "No!"

But nothing had prepared her for how fast that dog was. He leaped toward the counter, both paws up, scattering the kids, some of whom screamed.

"Tor!" Lucas and Pru both vaulted toward him, but her foot caught the metal gate on the puppy pen, knocking it over as she tumbled straight to the ground. She broke her fall with her backpack, looking up as Tor's big front paws managed to slam the tray of treats and flip the whole thing, sending them flying like a volcanic eruption of organic peanut butter dog bones all over the store and all over the now un-penned puppies.

Kids shrieked. Dogs barked. And the lady at the front looked like she wanted to kill somebody. Somebody named Pru.

In a flash, Lucas had captured Tor, who was chewing God knew how many treats. As Pru scrambled to her feet, she could hear Lucas apologizing to the cashier, but the high-pitched barks of puppies and a few of the customers' dogs joining in the madness were way louder.

"Get the puppies!" the woman from the front door hollered, making Pru realize that the gate had lifted high enough for them to scatter. "And you, get out!" she yelled at Pru.

"I'll help get the—"

"Out!" She pointed to the door. "With your boyfriend and your dog!"

"He's not—"

Lucas put his arm at her back, his other hand holding on to the leash to lead a still-chewing Tor. "Come on," he said. "They want us out of here."

"I know, but the—"

Suddenly, Tor stood at perfect attention.

"Whoa," Lucas said. "He wants to run. He has to run."

"No." Pru reached for the leash to add her weight to it.

Tor pulled, his gaze on something out in the mall. Who knew what could get his attention? Sniffing noisily, he pulled them toward the door, looking one way, then the other, smelling the ground as he went, stopping for the Christmas train and sniffing each car as it rolled by.

Finally, they managed to get him three stores away, and he walked to a bench, crawled under it, and dropped to the ground.

"His post-chaos nap," Pru said, only then catching her breath as she took a seat. "I'm so sorry, Lucas. I thought I had him and…"

"Don't sweat it." He sat on the bench, as spent as the dog. "He is totally out of control."

Below them, he snored.

For a second, they just looked at each other in dismay, then smiles pulled, and they both laughed from the bottom of their bellies.

"He's wild," Pru managed to say. "And then…" She pointed toward the sleeping dog. "This."

Still laughing, Lucas shook his head. "I really need some help with him."

"I think my dad could help you. Or my uncle Shane."

His laughter faded a little bit. "Thanks."

"Hey, that was my fault for taking my eye off the ball."

He put a hand on hers, his palm so big and warm she almost gasped out loud. "Are you okay? You fell."

"Not my most graceful moment."

"But you..." He gave her hand a squeeze. "You were awesome."

She stared at him for a moment, blinking, her mind blank except for one single thought.

Don't make me like you. Don't make me like you. Don't make me like you.

Still holding her hand, he stood, bringing her with him. "We better go find those grannies before they get into more trouble than Tor."

Oh snap. Too late. She liked him.

Chapter Six

"Are you hungry?" Finnie asked as she and Agnes slipped into plastic chairs at a table that gave them a direct view of Santa. He had two babies on his lap, one screaming, the other pulling his beard, while parents snapped photos. "There's a Greek place right there."

Agnes gave her an *are you serious?* look, then wrapped Pyggie and Gala's leashes around the leg of a chair at the next table, which was empty, but the slobs who'd sat there had left all their plates and plastic cups. Pyggie sniffed at the remnants, but knew well enough to settle on the cool tile floor under a chair at that table, so Agnes hooked her pocketbook on the empty chair above him.

"I know, I know." Finnie lifted the plastic lid to drop a tea bag in the wildly overpriced hot water from Starbucks. "'It's not Greek food if it's cooked by a pimply-faced teenage boy who doesn't know souvlaki from tzatziki.'" She somehow managed to lose the brogue when she imitated Agnes, but couldn't deliver a line with snark to save her sweet life. "Why are you putting your bag on that chair?"

59

"In the off chance it gets bussed, I don't want anyone sitting there."

"The dogs can be under our table. 'Tis quite crowded in here, and there aren't many empty tables."

"If someone sits there, it'll block my view of Aldo," she admitted. "And I still want to see what he's doing."

"Aye. Wouldn't want to miss his next hit job…on a blonde." Finnie grinned. "See what I did there?"

Agnes leaned in. "You *judged*," she said through gritted teeth. "The very thing you've been trying to drum out of me since the day we met."

Finnie's little shoulders dropped. "Aye, true."

"You think he's some kind of criminal because he has an Italian last name."

"No! I'm telling you my husband knew the man— or knew *of* him. He was part of a hunting club that Seamus belonged to years ago, and word was…he knew his way around the guns. Maybe a little too well, if you catch my drift."

"It was a *hunting* lodge." She rolled her eyes.

"But, oh, the ladies. Rumor was he had a different one every season."

"He told me he's been widowed for more than forty years. Can you blame the man for dating?"

"Dating women young enough to be his granddaughter?" Finnie tipped her head in the direction of Santa's Workshop. "Ye heard him with that lassie."

"I heard more than you did." And had seen the phone number exchange. "But I might have misunderstood. We can't assume he's all things bad until I get to know him. But I admit, it didn't look good." She let out a deep sigh. "I'm wasting my time, aren't I? There's no match for the matchmakers."

Finnie notched her chin. "Don't let yer coffee grow cold, lass." Then she put her hand over Agnes's, the soft, parchmentlike skin of her palm always a comfort. "Or yer heart. If it's love you want, then we'll find it for you."

"I don't expect anything like what we've managed to find for our grandchildren. Just a bit of the...magic. You know...the feeling? The roller coaster. The thrill."

"There's always Max Hewitt," Finnie said brightly. "He's keen on you, you know."

"I know, and he's a nice man, but..." Agnes closed hcr eyes. "You can't manufacture magic, and he's not..." *Intoxicating.* "I've always had a weakness for a man with a little spice and sizzle."

"Agnes. We're closer to ninety than nineteen. Leave the spicc and sizzle for Pru." She turned and looked into the crowd, then reached into her pocketbook to glance at her cell phone. "Where are those two, anyway? I hope that lad didn't have a wee bit *too* much sizzle, if you know what I mean."

"Is magic only for young people?" Agnes mused, stirring her coffee, watching the man who had yet another mother laughing. Although this time there was a father, too. So maybe he was just as charming as Santa as he was by text.

Finnie smiled. "We had our magic, lass. 'Tis a once-in-a-lifetime thing."

"Really? Then why live? I mean, does romance fade right along with good knees and a strong bladder? It's an age thing? That's just so sad and—"

She scowled as two men approached the next table and stared at the dogs. Gala barked, but Pyggie didn't move.

"Mind if we take this table?" one asked.

Yes, she did. "It's dirty." Agnes looked up at him and was met by an intimidating narrow-eyed stare.

"That's fine," the other man, a huge, beefy fellow with a beard, said. "We just need this seat."

And so did she. "There's a table over there by the Chinese food," she said. "Much more room and no dogs."

"I like dogs," the staring guy said, flipping her bag off the back of the chair and handing it to her. "Here you go, ma'am."

And down he went, with the house-size guy directly in front of Agnes, completely blocking her view. In fact, the two of them sat side by side, shoulder to shoulder, creating a veritable wall between Agnes and Aldo.

"Now I can't see him," she mouthed, frustrated as she shifted her seat to try to see through the space between the men's heads and shoulders.

"You're not missing anything," Finnie said.

"Except the very reason we're here."

Finnie tipped her head and pinned her blue gaze on Agnes. "What is the real reason we're here, dear friend? What are you searching for? Last year, 'twas the dog you'd seen in your dreams of heaven."

"It wasn't a dream," she whispered.

"And now it's the elusive man." Finnie pressed her hands together. "Is it the holidays that bring this out in you, Agnes? You spend so much time and money trying to look young and feel...*somethin'*. When you're surrounded by a beautiful family that gives you everythin'. Why are you searchin' so hard for happiness when, as we Irish say, you've got contentment knockin' at yer door?"

She had no answer for that, turning from Finnie's sincere gaze to try to see Aldo. But Big Guy leaned closer to Hard Eyes and blocked her view.

"I don't love that plan," Big Guy said. "It's not like we can walk right up to Santa and offer a bribe."

Wait, did he say *Santa*? And...*bribe*? Agnes glanced at Finnie, whose wide eyes showed she'd heard the same thing.

"But if he takes it," Big Guy said, "then what an FBI win we would have."

Agnes felt her jaw drop as she shared a shocked look with Finnie.

"I told you," Finnie mouthed.

Agnes shook her head to quiet her friend, inching closer.

"He has to take a break," Big Guy said. "I'm telling you, Sammy. That's when we go in for the kill."

The *kill*? Were they going to bribe him or kill him? Or kill him if he didn't take a bribe?

Sammy took out his phone and tapped the screen, and Finnie leaned around his other shoulder to see if she could read it, every bit as curious as Agnes was.

"I got his schedule here. Tony slipped it to me."

Finnie looked skyward—like just because someone named *Tony* was involved, that was proof positive they were dealing with mobsters. Of course, the mention of the FBI didn't exactly give Agnes a good feeling.

"His shift is done in fifteen minutes," Sammy said. "And he's not allowed to walk around in that costume, so he'll go right over there to the men's room and change. I say we get him in there, because then there shouldn't be any kids around."

Get him? Agnes bit her lip. What would they do to him with no kids around?

"You got the ghost?" Sammy asked.

Big Guy patted his jacket pocket, which bulged. "Oh yeah. And I'll put this sucker right under his nose and make him an offer even Aldo Fiore can't refuse."

Agnes and Finnie hissed in a breath at exactly the same time, making Gala jump and bark.

"Oh, did I bump her?" Big Guy said, turning in his chair to look at them. "Really sorry."

"No, no, 'tis fine," Finnie assured him in a reed-thin voice. "We're fine. No problem."

The man nodded and turned, while Sammy still studied his phone. "Did you see this?" he asked, angling the screen toward Big Guy. "Aldo's boys are busy."

Agnes inched closer, squinting at the screen, but seeing only the glare from the lights.

"Oh hell. That's a corpse. They found the damn corpse. We gotta get to Aldo, Sammy. This is a *crime*."

Agnes put her hand over her mouth, sharing a look with Finnie.

"We gotta step in here," Sammy said. "It's time for an FBI victory for a change. I'm sick of Fiore being so stinkin' elusive."

The two men both pushed up at the same time, their chairs noisily scraping the tile and waking Pyggie.

"Gosh, I'm sorry, little doggie." Big Guy leaned over, and his jacket—the one with the bulging pocket—opened when he leaned over to pet Pyggie. He wore a black T-shirt with a simple insignia on the pocket.

FBI.

Agnes just stared at him, holding her smile until they walked away in the direction of the men's room.

"Agnes!" All the color had drained from Finnie's face. "Do you believe me now?"

"I guess I do." She fell back in her chair. "How could I have been such a terrible judge of character?"

"Just be happy we found out the FBI is after him before you got involved with him."

Agnes nodded. "Is 'ghost' a slang term for a gun?"

"Of course it is!"

"Are you sure?" Agnes scowled, zipping through her memory. "I've never heard that."

"Neither have I, but did you see how his pocket was…" She made a bulging gesture with her hands. "And *corpse* is slang for a *corpse*, and *crime* means *crime*! Agnes, sweet Saint Patrick, you've dodged a bullet."

"Literally." She rubbed her hands together, only then realizing how cold she was. "What do you think they're going to do to him?"

"'Tis a sting," Finnie said with an amazing amount of authority for someone whose closest interaction with the FBI involved Efrem Zimbalist Jr. on a black-and-white TV screen.

"In the bathroom of the Vestal Village Mall on Christmas Eve?" It still seemed preposterous.

"Look around. There could be agents everywhere!"

Finnie gestured toward the crowded food court. "More men than you ever see at a mall."

"It's Christmas Eve," Agnes reminded her sharply. "That's when men shop."

"Why are you determined to protect and defend him?" Finnie asked, sounding flabbergasted.

"I'm not. But did those two guys really seem like FBI agents?"

"Undercover," Finnie said. "They're not supposed to look like FBI agents."

"They certainly didn't." Agnes shifted her gaze to Santa, who was waving to the kids and climbing off his throne.

"Ho, ho, ho! I gotta go! But I'll be back soon!" he called to them. "Watch the elves sing while I'm gone."

A ripple of disappointment as palpable as the one rolling through Agnes rumbled through the small crowd as he stepped off the small platform and headed directly toward them.

"Oh, he's coming here," Agnes exclaimed.

"No, no. Bathroom," Finnie corrected as Santa took a turn.

"Right into a sting." Agnes shook her head. "I feel like I should—"

"Agnes." Finnie grabbed her hand. "Just thank the good Lord you didn't fall for someone like that."

A little boy ran up to Santa, arms outstretched like he wanted a hug, and Aldo bent over and gave him a huge squeeze, lifting him in the air with a noisy, "Ho, ho, ho!"

"That doesn't look like a criminal," Agnes grumbled.

Another child came running over, then another. For at least ten minutes, Santa gave them hugs and encouragement and promised Santa would be back. With every passing second, Agnes began to doubt more and more what she'd heard.

"Are you ready to go, Agnes?" Finnie asked softly.

"Not until he walks into that bathroom and comes out in handcuffs," she whispered. "Then I'll give him up."

But just then, Santa turned in the other direction and walked right into the wide opening of a department store at the end of the mall.

"Where's he going?" Agnes asked, standing up.

"Penney's! He's getting away!" Finnie exclaimed. "We should tell the FBI men."

"You can." Agnes gathered the dogs' leashes and her bag. "Just waltz right into the men's room and look for the agents, Finola. See how that goes for you. I'm going to follow Aldo."

"Agnes!" Finnie sputtered, pushing up as well. "You can't."

"I can and I will. He's going into Penney's, Finnie. How much trouble can we get into there?"

"Speaking of trouble." Finnie put one hand on Agnes's arm and pointed with her other. "Here comes Tor, and...oh, look at that lassie and lad laughing."

Agnes couldn't resist an *I told you so* look. "I just had a feeling."

"Come on, let's go talk to them."

"Finnie! I'll lose him." She blew out a sigh. "Which is exactly what you want, isn't it?"

"What I want is for you to see straight where this awful man is concerned."

"Me, too. So let's follow him. And if he steals jewelry or does a drug deal or accepts a bribe, then I'll know."

"Gramma! Yiayia!" Pru called to them, and Gala tugged at her leash, eager to get to Pru.

"What will we tell them?" Finnie asked. "Can they go with us?"

Agnes watched the greyhound trot closer, his very presence catching every eye in the food court. "We'll be too conspicuous with that dog. They should stay here," Agnes said, glancing to see that Santa had been stopped by a kid again, giving her at least another moment.

"We've been looking all over for you," Pru said, a little breathless as she threaded through the tables to Agnes and Finnie, getting ahead of Lucas and Tor. "How's it going, you guys? Have you done any Santa stalking without me?"

"Not enough," Agnes said.

"Have you 'racked up' Random Acts of Christmas Kindness points, lass?"

"Not enough," Pru echoed. "But we were hoping to spread some cheer. And maybe get some food."

Agnes glanced over to see Santa waving at the last group of kids, still heading toward Penney's. "You stay and eat," she said, whipping out her wallet to throw twenty dollars on the table. "My treat. Take your time. Finnie and I are going—"

"He's wanted by the law!" Finnie burst out, just as Lucas and Tor reached the table.

"*What*?" The kids spoke in perfect unison, and Tor folded down next to Pyggie like he'd found a sleeping soul mate.

"Why did you tell them that, Finnie?" Agnes demanded.

"Because it's the truth," she fired back, her color high now, her Irish blue eyes lit like gas flames. "We overheard two gentlemen from the FBI planning to bribe him, then arrest him."

Pru's jaw dropped so hard it nearly hit the ground. "Are you kidding?"

"Who?" Lucas asked. "The Santa dude? The one right over there with the kids?"

Another group of youngsters had surrounded him, thank God, delaying his disappearance.

"Yes, that's him," Finnie said. "Aldo *Fiore*."

Agnes snorted. "You don't have to say his name like he's Satan himself, Finnie."

"Well, they said something about corpses and crime and a bribe. And a ghost! Isn't that another word for a gun?"

Lucas and Pru shared a look of utter confusion.

"Do you mean a Glock?" Pru asked.

"If ghost is a nickname for that," Agnes said. "Is it?"

"Hasn't reached California yet," Lucas told her.

"Whatever!" Agnes said. "I want to follow him."

"Why?" Again in unison.

"Because…" She looked from one to the other. "What better act of Christmas kindness than to help bring in a wanted Mafia boss? If we do that, Bitter Bark High School would win for sure."

Pru started to frown. "I don't know about that, Yiayia."

"She's right," Lucas said. "No way anyone's going to do anything bigger or better."

Finnie and Pru shared a look of silent communication, the connection of years and family and inbred caution easy to feel in the exchanged glance.

"'Tis a bad idea," Finnie said, adjusting her crooked glasses.

"Just to follow him?" Lucas asked. "How?"

"Thank you," Agnes said, her shoulders dropping in relief. "It looks like he's trying to get to Penney's."

"Where all hardened criminals hide," Pru joked.

"Finnie and I will follow him, and you stay here. With Tor. And the doxies." She shoved the leashes into Pru's hand. "There's money for your lunch. Oh, and watch the men's bathroom."

"Excuse me?" Pru asked on a dry laugh.

"Watch for two men who will be coming out," Agnes said. "One is about forty, with kind of hard, squinty eyes and a gray sweatshirt. That's Sammy. The other is very tall and large, wearing a navy blue jacket."

"With a bulge," Finnie said, leaning in to whisper, "'Tis his *ghost*."

The kids shared another look, just enough of a spark in their eyes to tell Agnes they weren't taking this seriously.

But Santa was almost completely out of the food court area, and there was no time for another word of explanation or persuasion.

"I'm going after him," Agnes announced, pushing a chair and anything else out of her way.

"Then I guess I am, too," Finnie said, right behind her.

"Gramma! Yiayia!"

But Agnes didn't wait to hear the rest or even turn when Gala panic-barked. After all the nice things Aldo had texted her this week, she was not going to just shrug and walk away.

If he was a criminal, then she was a fool.

If he was innocent, then she wanted to prove that.

Either way, she wanted to know the truth.

Chapter Seven

Pru dumped her backpack on the table as she sat, letting out a sigh. "Something tells me we are not really going to win the RACK IT UP contest."

"Winning's important to you, isn't it?" Lucas asked, smothering her in that intense gaze as he took a seat.

"I like to...achieve," she said, certain a guy like him would think that was completely lame. "I mean, it's better than losing."

"Guess it depends on what's at stake." He dropped his chin on his knuckles, looking hard at her. "Popularity? College? Attention? Validation? What ticks your boxes, Pru Kilcannon?"

Besides you? "Bancroft," she said softly, making him frown. "My last name is actually Bancroft."

"I'm sure I heard you called Pru Kilcannon at school."

"You talked about me to other kids?"

He leaned in a little, a smile deepening those dimples. "No, I don't talk to anyone, if you haven't noticed. But I heard about you. We're in a class together, remember?"

"But Mr. Thorgrim doesn't use my last name."

He shrugged. "I notice things about people who… attract my attention."

"Oh, that's…" An unexpected and unwelcome thrill danced through her, fluttering some of those butterfly wings. Dang. And she was just getting comfortable with him. "Interesting."

"You want to know why?"

Kind of more than anything. But she managed a shrug as she reached to open her bag, desperate for a distraction. "Probably because I'm the obnoxious kid in class who knows all the answers. Oh, look what I found. Dog treats."

Gala barked, Pyggie lifted his head, and Tor took two steps closer, so tall that he was almost eye to eye with her.

"Can I?" she asked Lucas.

"Of course."

She broke a Milk-Bone for Pyggie and Gala to share, then took out a whole one for Tor. "Can you sit?"

Lucas snorted. "All he can do is R-U-N."

"Ahhh. Well, let's learn to sit, okay?" She held the treat under his nose. "Down."

He stared at her but, to his credit, didn't try to eat it.

"Don't they train them with commands when they turn these dogs into racers?" she asked.

"He has commands. I just don't know them."

"Oh, like a *Schutzhund*," she said. "My uncle Liam trains German shepherds as four-legged bodyguards, and they have words that only they know. That way, a bad guy can't call your dog off, only you can." She studied him again, holding the dog's gaze, which was as magnetic as his owner's. "So you've never said a particular word, and he immediately stopped what he was doing?"

He shook his head. "I just say 'down' and 'stop' and 'oh crap, don't do that.'"

She laughed. "Well, we can try to give him new words. He'll be a breeze to train." She broke the Milk-Bone into three small pieces, then lowered a piece all the way to the floor, her grip on it tight, holding Tor's gaze. "Down, Tor."

After a second, he lowered his head toward the treat, but she held it back.

"Down, Tor."

"All the way, dude," Lucas said, encouraging him with a pat on his backside.

"No," Pru said. "The trick is to only use one word. The same word. And don't give him the treat until he does what you want on that word. Watch." She lifted the treat closer to his nose, the lowered it again. "Down, Tor."

After a second, he got down, and this time, he brought the rest of him along. Then Pru opened her hand and let him eat the bite from her palm. "Good boy!" she exclaimed. "Now let's do it again."

She repeated the whole process, finishing the Milk-Bone and half of another. After five straight successes, she pushed the remaining portion across the table to Lucas. "You try."

He took it down to the floor. "Down, Tor."

"Look into his eyes," she said.

Tor hesitated, but then lowered his whole body to the ground, getting the treat.

"That's good but he wants the treat," Lucas said, still obviously skeptical. "Not sure he's trained."

"Give it five minutes, then he gets a test." She gave Tor's head a good rub. "How long have you had him?"

"Not long at all. I just got him right before I left LA, and he was barely living in a house before that when my..." He swallowed. "My friend..." He shook his head.

Whoa, this girl had had an impact on him. "So you haven't had much time to train him," she said quickly, to help him out.

He gave her a quick, nearly imperceptible smile of gratitude. "No. And I don't know anything about his racing days or how old he is. Probably two? Maybe he raced, maybe he was retired because he couldn't win. There are thousands of greyhounds that need homes now that racing is being outlawed in most states."

"Thank God," she said. "It's inhumane. We've had a few come through my uncle's business, and they've all been sweet. Not quite this, uh, high-spirited, though."

He smiled down at Tor, who was resting again. "He's either on or off. There's no in-between."

"And when he's on," she joked. "Mall madness."

He laughed. "Don't even say that." They held each other's gazes for a second, then another, and suddenly...butterflies.

"So why do you have two last names, Pru?" he asked, the genuine interest in her making a few of those flying creatures dive-bomb. "'Cause your mom remarried?"

She sighed, looking down at the table and the twenty-dollar bill Yiayia had left, considering how easy it would be to simply offer to get food and not delve into her family history. Not that she was ashamed of her father, but it helped if a person had met him before they heard his background.

"It's kind of a complicated situation."

He gave a dry laugh. "These days? Whose isn't? Tell you what." He put his hand over hers, the touch light, but somehow still strong and reassuring. "You tell me your family mess, and I'll tell you mine."

"It's not a mess," she said quickly. "It's just...oh well. You'll hear it around school sooner or later."

"I'm intrigued." He scooted his chair a little closer, smiling. "And I promise I won't judge."

For a long moment, she looked at him, waiting for more butterfly shenanigans in her belly. But the feeling inside her wasn't quite as nervous anymore, or even excited. Now she felt something completely different. More like friendship, but different. A connection, a budding trust, and oh yeah, all kinds of attraction.

Suddenly, she very much wanted to share her story, if only to see his reaction. Some people recoiled. Some people pitied. And yeah, plenty of people judged.

"My dad was in prison for fourteen years, and I didn't meet him until he got out."

His brows lifted. "Not what I would have guessed from the future valedictorian."

Wow, he *had* been paying attention to her in school. "I was as surprised as anyone," she said. "And he was in for...manslaughter."

"You were surprised? You didn't know where he was?"

For some reason, she liked that he didn't react to *manslaughter*. "I didn't know who he was," she admitted. "I was raised by a single mom who was very discreet and quiet about my father."

"Because he was in prison?" he guessed.

"She had no idea he was there," she told him. "He stopped a man from attacking a woman in a parking lot when he was working as a bouncer at a bar. He accidentally pushed the guy, who hit his head and died. He didn't, you know, set out to kill anyone. But my mom didn't know any of this."

"She didn't wonder where he was?"

"They didn't really know each other," she admitted. "It was a one-night stand. In the back of a van designed for hauling around foster dogs."

His eyes flashed, and that almost-smile threatened. "The dog thing runs deep, huh?"

She laughed with him, ridiculously pleased with the complete lack of judgment in his response. "But long story short? He showed up in Bitter Bark after he got out, needed a vet, hired my mom, and now…" She beamed at him. "They're married, happy, and I have a baby brother named Danny."

His jaw loosened. "Wow. That's cool."

She really loved that response. "Yeah, it is." She glanced around, remembering that they were supposed to be RACKing up points and watching for FBI agents on a sting…not sitting here like they were *on a date*. "We forgot to watch for the guys coming out of the bathroom," she reminded him.

"Totally distracted." His look was a little smoky,

but charming, too. Nothing like…well, like she expected. "But they haven't come out." He nodded toward the restroom entrance behind her. "I'm keeping an eye out for them. And what's next on your RACKing list? Sing a few carols? Hand out free bottles of water?"

"I guess we could…" She reached for her bag, then stopped and looked at him. "Wait. You promised to tell me your family story if I told you mine."

"Oh yeah." He waved it off. "That's not going to get us any points."

"You're not in this for points," she said, studying him openly. "You need a community service hour or two to finish the semester."

"Guilty, but now I'm all in. Let's RACK, Kilcannon. Or, Bancroft."

She smiled. "Okay…Darling." As soon as she said it, she felt the warmth of a blush creep up her cheeks, and he laughed easily.

"That's not my name," he admitted. "So we have that in common."

"It's not?" She shook her head. "Then why…"

"My dad's real last name is Dildenberg. Stop laughing right now."

She bit her lip. "That is…unfortunate."

"He was an actor back in the eighties, and his agent made him change his name for obvious reasons, and they came up with Darling since he was supposed to be, you know, the next Leo DiCaprio or George Clooney."

"Did he get famous?" she asked.

"Not as an actor. And not really famous, because no one knows the producers outside of the Hollywood circles, but yeah. He's made movies I guarantee you've heard of."

"And your mom?"

"She remarried and now she's a...professional wife." He made a face like there was way more to that story.

"Is your dad remarried?"

"No, he just has a harem of wannabe actresses." He rolled his eyes. "Never knew who I'd find in the kitchen when I came down for breakfast."

"You live with your dad? I would have thought your mom."

"He's the lesser of two evils," he explained. "And my mom travels with her husband, who is..." He leaned in and looked from one side to the other. "The drummer for Split Second."

"The band? *The* Split Second? My dad loves their music." A slow smile formed as she put a few puzzle pieces together. "So your father *is* a rock star."

"Stepfather, who I barely speak to."

"Wow. So, what's so messy? I mean, lots of people have divorced and remarried parents."

"The mess is money," he said without a second's hesitation. "Money—at least the kind they both have—makes people messy. And stupid. And mean. And careless. And..." His voice trailed off as he shifted his gaze over her shoulder. "Could that be the FBI agents?"

She turned, saw two men, and assessed them. "They meet the description."

"Let's watch where they go." He shifted his chair, one hand sliding into Tor's collar as if he half expected the dog to run after the two men.

But when the men went to the line for Chick-fil-A and ordered, Pru and Lucas leaned back and shared a look.

"Should we go tell them their target went to Penney's?" he asked.

"I don't know." Pru shook her head and scanned the mall for any sign of the grannies. "Gramma and Yiayia have been known to make mistakes in their, uh, interpretation of things."

"The Dogmothers?" He chuckled. "I love that they have a team name."

"They're matchmakers," she said. "And they claim many committed relationships, including several marriages and one set of twins on the way."

"Matchmakers?" He choked a laugh. "They still exist?"

"In my family," she said, shaking her head and hoping he didn't put two and two together and come up with...*Prucas*. God help her. She propped her chin on her palm. "So, you just moved yourself to Bitter Bark from Los Angeles? You weren't, like, sent here as punishment?"

"Contrary to public opinion, I was not escaping the long arm of the law, or forced to do community service for my misdeeds, or part of a gang, or whatever gossip you heard."

"But some rumors were right. Or close, at least."

He rolled his eyes. "The truth is, my dad told me if I wanted to keep this dog, I had to move out."

"What?" She blinked at him.

He shrugged. "He'd been looking for a way to get rid of me ever since one of the harem thought I should join in their fun."

She drew back, slightly horrified. "Now that one hasn't hit the rumor mill."

"I declined," he said quietly. "I really am shy. And kind of not into...that. Anyway, Tor and I took off the next day."

"To stay with your aunt and uncle...*ish*."

He looked like he was about to say more, then reconsidered it, shifting his attention to the sleeping dog next to him. "Has it been five minutes? Can we test his skills?"

"Sure." She handed Lucas a treat, and instantly Tor was up, looking at the Milk-Bone. "Remember what word to use. Only once and his name."

He nodded and held the treat just out of reach. "Down, Tor."

Tor blinked, but didn't move.

"Down," Lucas repeated. "And...nothing."

"Attention! Attention!" They both spun around at the order from a man in a red jacket marching through the tables, holding out flyers like he was selling newspapers.

"Isn't that the cashier from the pet store?" Pru asked.

"Yup."

"We have a missing puppy from The Animal House pet store! If you see this dog or someone with this dog, he needs to be returned ASAP."

Lucas and Pru shared a look of dismay, but before they could say a word, the man spotted them—well, he spotted Tor.

"Nice work, you two," he muttered, slapping a flyer with a photocopy of a dog's picture on it. "Buttercup was either stolen or lost in that mess you created."

Pru sucked in a breath when she recognized the basset puppy who had captivated Tor's attention. "Oh gosh, that's horrible."

The cashier—although the name badge he wore said David, Manager—just shot Lucas a dark look. "I should have known you were up to no good with that whole random-act-of-kindness crap. For all I know, you arranged to steal Buttercup. That basset is worth a lot of money on the street."

Lucas just looked away, his expression blank.

But incredulity and fury shot through Pru. "Excuse me? You're accusing him of stealing a dog?"

"Probably stole this one," the guy said, glancing at Tor.

"He's *a racing rescue.*" Pru practically sputtered the words. "Why would you even suggest such a thing?"

The guy gave her a *get real* look and threw another one of pure disgust at Lucas. "Just stay the hell away from my store," he said. "We don't need any more trouble." With that, he pivoted, then turned back to fire one more parting shot. "Someone was supposed to get that dog today, and you wrecked their Christmas!"

At the vicious tone, Tor dropped right to the ground, his head down, eyes up. Pru leaned over to rub his back, sympathy welling up for how he reacted when the man yelled.

"Lucas," she said, watching how he looked away, too, very much like the dog. "Are you going to just sit there and let him accuse you of stealing dogs?"

He shrugged. "People suck."

"And need to be corrected."

"Pru, chill." He ran a hand through his long, unruly

hair. "I'm used to it. People assume the worst." He leaned forward. "Didn't you?"

She held his gaze for a long time, almost unable to look away. "Did. Past tense. All it took was about an hour of talking to you to see I was wrong."

He let out a soft sigh, barely audible over the din of the food court, then stood. "Shouldn't we be doing something kind?" he asked, picking up the twenty-dollar bill. "I think I'll go buy someone's lunch. Be sure to get a picture. Otherwise, no one will believe I'm capable of it."

He took off with Tor, leaving her with the doxies and a whole lot of questions. And some serious shame for ever assuming the worst of someone who was actually more than a pretty face. A lot more.

Chapter Eight

"He moves fast for an old guy," Finnie said from behind Agnes's shoulder.

"No, you move slow," Agnes grumbled, keeping her gaze locked on the man in the red and white Santa outfit headed toward an escalator. "Where the hell is he going in Penney's?" she murmured under her breath.

"Agnes." Finnie underscored the warning with a gentle but firm hand, a touch Agnes recognized so well. She was trying to smooth out Agnes's rough edges, which was normally appreciated, but Agnes was too frustrated by the day to appreciate anything.

"You really don't want me to have any fun, do you, Finnie?"

"If by 'fun' you mean swearing and mocking my old legs that don't move quite like they used to, then no."

Aldo was stuck behind a group on the escalator, so Agnes took a second to turn, ready to sling back a comment that bubbled up from deep inside. But one look in those Irish blue eyes, and the volcano suddenly quieted.

And that was Finola Kilcannon's secret power.

"I'm sorry, Finnie," she said on a sigh. "It's my nerves and disappointment, I guess. I thought he was going to be…wonderful."

Finnie's tiny shoulders dropped, and the fight went out of her at the same time. "Maybe he *is* wonderful, Agnes. Maybe we didn't hear that whole business correctly."

"But I'm afraid we did."

"Donchya be worryin', lass." She gave a light nudge to Agnes's shoulder. "If he gets off that escalator, and we lose him, we'll never forgive ourselves. Haul your butt, Greek grandmother."

Agnes snorted a soft laugh, a familiar affection welling up. "Okay, then hold my arm, and let's power through the crowds."

They did, parting people like Moses at the Red Sea, until they were about twenty feet behind him.

"He has fine shoulders," Finnie whispered as they gazed at him.

"And a fine Santa rear under all that fur."

They both giggled their way to the top of the escalator, spotting him heading to the Men's Department, threading his way around tables of wallets and belts, all the way to the Customer Service Department.

"Bathroom?" Finnie guessed.

"Could have used the one downstairs," Agnes said. "But—oh, look."

A man came up to him, holding a shopping bag, stopping to talk. They were too far away to hear anything, but Agnes studied the man who didn't look much older than any of her grandsons. He had dark hair, a gray hooded sweatshirt, and leaned in to talk to Aldo.

After a moment, he gave Aldo the shopping bag, chuckled about something, then shook his head as he walked away. Aldo headed toward the Customer Service entry, disappearing around a corner.

"'Twas a handoff," Finnie said. "Drug deal? Money laundering?"

"Maybe a change of clothes?" Agnes suggested, since Finnie had clearly lost her mind.

"So he can slip out unnoticed by the feds."

The feds? "You've been reading too many suspense novels, Finola."

Not five minutes later, as they pretended to be fascinated by a selection of underwear, he stepped out, dressed head to toe in street clothes—which fit his tall frame rather nicely—the shopping bag gone.

Agnes exchanged a look with Finnie, and Finnie's eyes were sparking with horror.

"What?" Agnes demanded. "He can't walk around dressed as Santa! The kids will attack him. He gets a lunch break, for heaven's sake."

"Or he's undercover."

"He's simply...taking a phone call." She yanked Finnie behind a tall display of tighty-whities, hiding as he put his phone to his ear and walked closer to them. "Hush up, Finola!"

She could hear a low laugh as he approached. "Well, I'm telling you I found her. She's the one. Young, beautiful. Has a kid, but really, who cares? At this point, I can't be picky."

Now Agnes was sure her expression was as horrified as Finnie's.

"I got her number, too."

Agnes closed her eyes, punched in the gut by the words. And how nice his voice was. Why did he have to have a nice voice? And hair that was thicker and even shinier than in his picture? Why couldn't he be schlumpy and bald?

"Well, now I shop," he said. "Oh yeah, I know they're here. FBI all over the place. Ever since they saw the corpse, there's no getting rid of those guys."

Agnes caught herself from gasping, pressing her hand to her mouth as he passed by, hearing Aldo's easy laugh. At the FBI! He was certainly…fearless.

"I have plenty of time to shop," he said. "Look, I have someone special, and I want to impress the hell out of this woman…" He got too far away for them to hear the rest, but Finnie turned to her, her eyes bright with emotion.

"It's all true!" she exclaimed. "The FBI! The corpse!"

"The woman he wants to impress the hell out of." Agnes let out a sigh, an age-old regret crawling up her chest, taking her back many, many years to another really bad decision she made because a man was handsome. "I sure can pick 'em, can't I?"

"We have to help the FBI find him," Finnie said. "We can't let him sail out of here and get away with murder! It's our civic duty!"

"Finnie, we can't—"

"We must! Look! He's headed back to the escalator. Let's follow." She yanked Agnes's arm, her little legs hustling down the shiny tile floor. But Agnes just didn't have it in her to go running off on this adventure.

For a person who'd made passing judgment on others into an Olympic sport, how could she have *mis*judged him so completely? He'd seemed so genuine and real.

On a sigh, she followed, but stayed ten feet behind Finnie, who marched on her rubber-soled shoes like a woman on a mission.

At the bottom of the escalator, he paused, looked left, then right, and then powered toward the accessories like a man who didn't have a care in the world or a cop on his tail.

Finnie followed, stopping next to him at a display of silk scarves.

As Finnie sidled up to him, Agnes stayed back, hovering behind a rack of handbags so he wouldn't see her, but she could hear.

"What do you think?" He turned to Finnie and held up two scarves. "Which would you prefer?"

She sputtered a little, obviously not expecting the question. She adjusted the crooked glasses, then shrugged. "I imagine it depends on the woman."

He sighed. Actually let out a true, wistful sigh. "Then whichever one is prettier, I guess. She is."

"Oh, then..." Finnie reached for the one in his right hand. "I prefer this one a wee bit more, then, for a pretty lass."

"Yeah, but it's kind of long, isn't it? I mean, what could you do with all this? Tie someone up?" He laughed, but Agnes gulped.

"I'm sure I wouldn't know," Finnie said, suddenly preoccupied with other scarves.

"Irish or Scottish? I hear some lilting brogue in your voice."

"Irish," she said tightly.

"I'm Italian," he replied. "Well, my ancestors are. It sounds like you're the real deal."

"I am," she answered.

"What about this one?" He held up a fuchsia infinity scarf. "Too pink?"

"Too…" Finnie stepped back and looked up at him. "For your wife?" she asked, an edge in her voice.

"Oh God, I wish she was my wife. Maybe she will be someday."

"If you make her an offer she can't refuse."

Agnes nearly choked.

But Aldo laughed heartily. "I see what you did there, since I'm Italian. Very funny, ma'am. The only thing I don't want her to refuse is my gift." He hung the scarf in its place. "Maybe perfume? Earrings? Too much? I really want to impress her."

Who was this woman he wanted to impress? That child with a child of her own? He just didn't strike her as a playboy. Irritation skittered up her spine as she remembered the young mother he'd been flirting with. And his voice on the phone when he'd said he found *the one* and got her number.

"Well, how well do you know her?" Finnie asked, engaging him in conversation for reasons Agnes would never understand.

"Not that well," he admitted on a laugh. "I'm not even sure if a present is appropriate, but with the holidays, it seemed right."

"Maybe just some simple flowers," Finnie said.

Why was she giving him advice?

He laughed again. A rich, from-the-chest laugh that Agnes wished she didn't like so much. "That might be a little, oh, I don't know, unimaginative."

"All women like flowers," she said.

"But flowers are my business. I get them for free."

"Well, then ye should know that women love flowers. Pick one that reminds you of her—a red rose or a white orchid—and tell her why that flower reminds you of her, and that will impress her more than a scarf."

"Clever. What's your name?"

Oh, now he was hitting on Finnie? Agnes inched her head to the side to see the exchange rather than just hear it.

"Finola." She extended her hand.

"That's a fine Irish name," he said, smiling down at her as he shook her hand. "I'm Aldo. And it was nice chatting with you."

"Aren't you going to get the scarf for your lady friend?" she asked.

"I think I'll take your advice and get her a flower. I want it to be special, because she is." He gave a nod. "Merry Christmas, Finola."

He walked away, leaving both of them behind. Agnes stepped out from her hiding place behind the handbags.

"What happened to turning him in?" she asked.

"I was just trying to get a read on the man," Finnie said.

"And what did you *read*?"

Finnie looked in the direction he'd gone. "He does seem…I don't know. Not like a mobster."

"Oh, now he's not a mobster. Now that he's got some hussy on the line and the FBI down his throat. *Now* you like him?"

Finnie sighed. "I wouldn't say I like him, but if I

hadn't heard him talking about the FBI and a corpse with my own ears…" She shook her head. "Come on, Agnes. We can't lose sight of him."

"So we can turn him in for the good of our community," Agnes said glumly.

Finnie slipped her arm around Agnes's. "So what did you think of him, seeing him up close and not dressed as Santa for the first time?"

"That he posted a real picture, because he is handsome. Tall. Warm." She made a face. "Also buying a scarf for 'the one' who is young, beautiful, and has a kid, but he doesn't care because he can't be picky."

Silently, they walked out of the store, pausing at the big entrance to the mall, not far from the massive tree and the hordes of people around Santa's Workshop.

"Did we lose him?" Finnie asked, looking left and right. "Did he go up those stairs?"

"Let's look." They walked to the large, curved stairs and climbed them to the top, heading to the railing for a direct view down to the holiday heart of the mall. Silent for a moment, they scanned the people, trying to spot Aldo.

Then a loud shriek echoed over the sound of carolers, followed by a bark. A familiar bark.

"Is that Gala?" Agnes pushed farther over the railing to see down, her heart leaping as more shrieks floated up, searching the crowds.

"Oh dear." Finnie grabbed her arm and pointed. "'Tis Tor!"

"I don't see…" She sucked in a breath at the sight of the toppled pile of wrapped boxes and Tor running down the mall through the crowds with a giant gold ribbon in his mouth. Behind him, Lucas tried to catch up, calling his name.

Next to the presents, Pru stood with the doxies on leashes, both of them barking, all of them watching helplessly.

"We best go down there," Finnie said.

"Yes, but, Finnie, look!" She pointed to the entrance to the food court, where the two FBI men from earlier came marching out, side by side. The big one had his hand in his bulging pocket, like he would draw out a gun at any minute.

"And there's Aldo," Finnie said, gesturing to the wide, curved stairs they'd just climbed. He was walking slowly, but then he froze and stared across the crowded mall, and instantly his whole body changed.

"He sees them," Agnes said.

"But they don't see him."

Aldo pivoted, darting up the stairs with surprising speed and agility for a man of his age. But then, fear of the law could probably do that to someone.

He made it to the top, then blew right by them, the phone at his ear.

"FBI Mayday," they heard him say. "Would you please get these knuckleheads off my back before I kill someone?"

Agnes squeezed the railing, taking a steadying breath.

"Come on, lass," Finnie said gently. "You know what we have to do."

Chapter Nine

If Pru hadn't noticed that both the grannies looked flushed and upset as they approached, she would still have known something was wrong by the way Gala reacted. Pyggie was unfazed, as always, sniffing around the mall floor for a random morsel of food.

But sensitive little Galatea began to whine even before Gramma Finnie and Yiayia reached them, tapping her paws on the tile, anxious and stressed at the sight of them.

"You're not going to believe what happened," Pru said as she bent over to lift the doxie and give her a kiss before handing her over to Yiayia.

"We saw, lass," Gramma Finnie said, looking around as if she was more interested in the crowd than anything else. "Where did they go?"

"Tor took off, and Lucas followed." Pru pointed down the wide mall corridor, packed now with last-minute shoppers. "We were trying to come up with some kind of Random Act of Christmas Kindness so we didn't completely waste the day. We got closer to the workshop, and Tor started sniffing around the boxes, then he dug into the pile, knocked it over, and almost took half the tree with him. Then he grabbed a ribbon off a box and took off like, well, a racing dog."

"No!" Yiayia said, still looking around.

"Yes," Pru replied.

"I don't mean what happened to *him*." Yiayia finally focused on Pru, her dark eyes as desperate as Tor's when he'd launched at that pile of presents. "I mean the FBI men. They were headed to the stairs. Did they go up?"

"I don't know."

"You were *supposed* to watch. Did you forget?"

Gala lifted her little snout and gave Yiayia's chin a comforting lick, recognizing that raised voice of panic and reminding Pru not to snap back.

"I'm sorry," Pru said softly.

"'Tis fine, lassie." Gramma Finnie came around Pru's other side to give her a great-grandmotherly hug. "You were distracted. Agnes is just upset."

Yiayia's shoulders dropped as she heaved a sigh. "Nothing about today is going as planned," she admitted.

"Well, what did you think was going to happen, Agnes?" Finnie asked. "You'd lock eyes with the man, and he'd go down on one knee? I told you his reputation precedes him, and now we have a new mission. To get him behind bars where he belongs."

Pru threw a look at Gramma Finnie. "You're not entirely sure of that," she said, slipping into her automatic role as peacemaker on the rare occasion things got tense between these two.

"Not to mention that you insisted poor Pru get a boyfriend out of what should have been a day at the mall." Gramma Finnie's cheeks grew bright with two patches of red. "And the boy is nothing but trouble, along with his dog."

"Gramma!" Pru drew back. "What is wrong with you?"

Gala felt it, too, squiggling to get out of Yiayia's grip to turn her sympathetic kisses to her other owner.

"I'm telling you, she's jealous," Yiayia said.

"And I'm telling you..." But Gramma Finnie couldn't finish the sentence, looking from one to the other, finally letting out a sigh as her blue eyes filled with tears and what Pru recognized as a rare display of shame. "I'm just hungry. Can we get some food and take a break from all this...arguin'?"

"Amen to that," Pru said, putting her hands on both the grannies' backs and leading them toward the food court. "Let's regroup, remind each other that it's Christmas, and figure out how I can possibly salvage this afternoon with some RACK points."

They reluctantly followed as she leaned in to whisper to both of them, "A boyfriend, Yiayia? Seriously?"

"I see sparks between you," she said on a bitter-sweet laugh. "Don't I?"

Sparks? Was that what was flying between Pru and Lucas? "Well, he's not awful like I thought," Pru said. "But that's all I'll commit to."

The two older ladies shared a look, conspiratorial enough that Pru relaxed a little. She didn't want to be one of the victims of their matchmaking, but she sure didn't want them at odds, so she just let it go.

A few minutes later, they were settled at another table with a view of another Santa—this one was much younger—with some food and drinks and still no sign of Lucas and Tor.

Pru pushed down the tendril of disappointment that came with that thought. "Maybe he and Tor took an Uber and bailed," she said a little glumly. "Can't say I'd blame him."

"He's not going anywhere," Yiayia said, her gaze scanning the area. "I can tell by the way he looks at you."

"At me?" Pru let out a nervous laugh.

"Can't argue with her, lass," Gramma Finnie said.

"Good, because I can take anything but you two fighting. Now tell me everything that happened while you were in Penney's."

She listened while they took turns filling her in on the man you'd think was at the top of the FBI's most-wanted list to hear them describe it.

"Are you guys sure it's really the FBI, and this is a sting?" Pru sipped her soda, fighting a smile. "Because it's a little…far-fetched."

"I wish we were wrong," Yiayia said. "I wish I hadn't heard him say there are 'FBI all over the place.'"

"And then he said," Gramma leaned in to whisper, "'Ever since they saw the corpse, there's no getting rid of those guys.' And that he was going to kill someone!" Her eyes widened. "Does that sound like we're imagining things?"

"No, but you are both in your eighties," she reminded them gently. "And maybe you didn't hear exactly what was said."

"Then why did he run from them?" Yiayia asked, gesturing toward the stairs. "And why…oh, here's your boyfriend. I knew he'd come back, Pru."

"He's not my…" She turned to see Lucas and Tor coming toward them, his long hair brushed back from how quickly he was walking, his jacket in one hand, the leash in the other. Tor looked particularly repentant, and Lucas looked particularly…hot.

He spotted her and jutted his chin in a distant greeting, the hint of a smile lifting his lips and a spark—just like the ones Yiayia claimed to see—in his brown eyes.

Boyfriend.

Wow. If she ever got one, he'd look like *that* in a black T-shirt.

"Ladies." He reached the table, flipped a plastic chair around, and straddled it to face them. "We have a problem."

"Not another one," all three answered in unison, making him laugh softly, and suddenly it was like all was right in Pru's world. The one that felt a little tilted and dizzy when she looked at him.

"But I actually think Tor is going to fix this one instead of cause it," he told them, inching in closer. "The missing puppy?"

"*What* missing puppy?" Gramma Finnie demanded.

Pru reached over to the next table and grabbed a flyer. "This one. Buttercup."

"A sweet basset," Finnie crooned, sharing it with Yiayia. "Look, Agnes. This little angel somehow escaped from the pet store."

"Somehow," Pru and Lucas both said on a groan, sharing a secret look.

"How can Tor fix this problem?" Yiayia asked. "Assuming that's the problem you mean."

"Tor's on this puppy's trail," he said. "That's why he jumped into the boxes. Someone saw him there. And then when he ran? Well, the puppy got away and was spotted in the play area."

"Why doesn't someone just get him and take him back to the pet store?" Pru asked.

"He's a wily little thing, and most people must think he belongs to someone else. By the time they figure out he's loose and lost, he's gone. But he's out there, and Tor's gonna find him. He *has* to."

"Why?" Pru asked, sensing an undercurrent of desperation in his voice.

He looked from one side to the other before leaning in to say, "Because some people from the local paper are here, and a manager from the pet store pointed me out as the culprit, and if we don't get that puppy back…" He sighed. "Then the FBI in this place will be coming after me and not your Santa friend."

"What?" Pru practically choked on her soda. "You mean the guy who was such a jerk and who accused you when he was here?"

"That's the one, the assistant manager of The Animal House, heady with power. He's putting the blame on me. Claims I was 'distracting' him with the RACK things while Tor pushed over the fence. He hasn't said it was on purpose, but that's the impression he's happy to give."

The injustice of it practically rocked Pru. "I was holding Tor!" She tapped the table in frustration. "I should be the one in trouble."

"Gee, Pru, look at you. Look at me. Who do you think they're going to blame?"

She pushed up from her seat, nearly sputtering. "Well, I am going to—"

He reached across the table and put his hand on hers, the heat of his palm nearly taking her breath away. "*We* are going to walk every inch of this mall and let Tor help us find the puppy. And then we'll return him to The Animal House pet store."

"And if we don't find him?"

He blew out a breath. "I promised I'd pay for him."

"*We* will pay for him," Pru said. "You can't be on the hook for this, Lucas. It wasn't your fault. How much is the dog?"

He gulped. "Five hundred dollars."

Pru blinked at him, the amount making her fall right back into her chair. "Seriously?"

He stood, still holding her hand. "I wish I was kidding. Come on, Kilcannon Bancroft. We got work to do."

She stood with him, looking down at one granny and then the other. "Do you mind if we…"

"Go, lass. You must do all you can to straighten out this mess."

"But what about your RACK points?" Yiayia asked.

"I'm afraid that's a lost cause," Pru said. "I mean, what can we do, hand out dollar bills as we walk? We tried that in the pet store, and it only got us in trouble."

"Wait!" Gramma Finnie grabbed her bag. "I know what you can do! Not sure if it's a winning strategy, but…" She fished through her bag and pulled out a pack of red and green Post-it Notes, many of the pages folded.

"Your idea pad, Gramma?"

"'Tis the holiday edition," she said with a yellowed grin. "I've been writing down my favorites for the whole month. You can post them all over the mall, and someone's day is sure to be brightened."

Pru smiled at her. "That's sweet, Gramma, but—"

Tor started pulling at his leash just as a high-pitched whistle echoed through the whole mall. Tor barked and yanked.

"He wants to get on Santa's train," Lucas said. "Come on, it's a start."

Pru gave him an *are you serious?* look, then tossed another look to the grannies. "Should I…"

"On with ye, lass." Gramma stuffed the notes in her hand. "Find the puppy. Post some happy notes. Save yourselves five hundred dollars! We'll just stay here and wait for Al Capone."

Laughing—because how could she do anything else?—and still holding Lucas's hand, Pru took off with him for the Christmas train, with Tor leading the way.

Chapter Ten

Finnie fussed with the lid of her cup, her gaze down, her narrow shoulders tense. Under her chair, Gala panted lightly, then dropped her chin on Finnie's rubber-soled shoe.

"Your mood is rubbing off on Galatea," Agnes said.

"It is?" Finnie looked up, clearly pulled out of her thoughts, then reached down to the little dog. "Sweet lassie," she murmured. "It's not healthy to be quite as sensitive as you are."

"So you don't deny that you're upset?"

"'Tis a complicated day," she said, looking around. "And I'm a wee bit tired from the runnin' about."

"You? Tired? You never get tired."

She gave a sad smile. "I do my best to keep up with you, Agnes."

Something shifted in Agnes's chest. Something that shifted a lot with this woman. Something that, honestly, before she met Finola Kilcannon, rarely had shifted at all.

"What's wrong?" Agnes leaned in and put a hand on Finnie's slightly knotted fingers, not surprised that they were as tense as her shoulders.

Finnie blinked in surprise. "I think the real question is, 'What's right?'" She let out a light, not very genuine, laugh. "'Tis a day of upheaval and frustration, and on Christmas Eve, no less."

"We agreed we would come and check him out, Finnie."

"And we did," she said. "And now we're waitin' to turn him in to the authorities. Poor Pru is on the hook for a lot of money, and instead of finishing up our wrappin' and cookie bakin', we're in a crowded mall."

It wasn't what she was saying that concerned Agnes, it was the tone. "I think I can count on one hand the times I've heard you be less than positive and enthusiastic, Finnie. I am..." She swallowed. Hard. "I'm sorry I dragged us here today. Let's leave the minute the kids come back."

"Oh." Finally, Finnie looked right at her, and her eyes filled with tears.

"What? What's wrong, Finnie?"

"I don't know." Her voice cracked as she shook her head. "I just don't know what to be thinkin' anymore."

Agnes scanned her friend's face, looking for a way to read into these words. Every little crinkle and change of expression in her face was so familiar after nearly two years of being inseparable, but she simply couldn't remember ever seeing this look of...sadness.

"Finnie, I had no idea this was going to upset you so. If I had, we wouldn't have come."

"It's not...today. It's..." She waved a hand and blinked back her tears. "'Tis the season, I suppose." She added a laugh and tried to sound bright and cheery, but failed miserably. "Why don't you take a walk around and see if you can find your Aldo, and I'll watch for—"

"He's not my Aldo," Agnes interjected. "He's some criminal, and I should have listened to you."

"Fine, he's not yours. But Max was interested in you—"

"I told you I have no interest in Max Hewitt other than as a friend."

"Then it will be...the next one." She sighed and managed a smile. "One of them will win your heart."

For a moment, Agnes didn't say a word, still processing just what was going on in her friend's mind. "You know, every time I've said you're jealous, I haven't meant it. I was joking."

"I'm not jealous."

"I know," she said. "You're one of the rare—no, no, you are the *only* female friend I've had since being a widow who wasn't a little jealous of me. That group down in Florida that I socialized with at the apartment complex? Every time I lost a pound or got a new round of Botox or had my hair colored, they judged me. I heard it in their comments, felt it in their looks. But worse, they judged themselves. My wanting to be attractive no matter my age drove a wedge between other women and me. But that has never happened with you."

"Those things aren't important to me, but I respect that they are to you."

Agnes didn't respond, still studying Finnie and trying to figure out where all this emotion was coming from, since it wasn't jealousy.

"I'm...scared," Finnie whispered, so softly the

words could barely be heard over the din of shoppers and Christmas carols.

"Of what?"

"Of *losin'* you."

Agnes stared at her. "You think you're going to lose me?"

"Of course I am. When the right man comes along, he'll see what I see."

"What you see?" Agnes shook her head. "I don't follow."

"All the things that make you so lovely, lass." She gave a sad smile. "You'll make him laugh at your quick wit and convince him to take chances he never dreamed of takin', and then you'll have your secret jokes and nicknames for people."

"Like we do," Agnes whispered, the words making Finnie's eyes fill again.

"Aye, like I haven't had with anyone else since…Seamus." She tried to swallow, but that just made the tears she was fighting slip out and meander over the creases in her cheeks. "The truth is, lass, you've made my life so full and fun, so different and exciting again, that I'm bone-deep terrified of livin' without you."

The words landed like a punch to Agnes's chest, hitting that sweet spot that was saved for so few people. Just Nik, really, and now Finnie.

"I'm never going to leave you, Finn," she promised, squeezing Finnie's hand to show how much she meant those words. "You're the first and best and most real woman friend I've ever had. I walked into that wedding shower for my former daughter-in-law and your son that day, and I could feel every single person in that room tense up because I arrived. My own grandchildren were more than a little afraid of me."

Finnie smiled. "They were," she agreed.

"But you took me in as your friend. You put your little cardigan-wearing arm around my shoulders and gave me the ultimate Gramma Finnie blessing."

She laughed softly. "I liked ye the minute I met ye."

"Finnie, no one says that about me."

"Then they're missing out," she declared. "Yes, you have sharp edges, but you also have vivid color and big ideas and the ability to make the most mundane activity feel like an adventure."

Now Agnes felt tears rise. "I do?" Had anyone ever taken the time to see all that in her? Certainly no other woman she'd ever met. "But you've made me better, Finnie. So much better."

"Aye, you're a work in progress," she joked. "But I'm not ready to quit, and I know my days with ye are numbered."

"Finnie, we'll always be friends. And family, now. No matter what. Nothing and no one can change that."

Finnie tipped her head and lifted a dubious white brow. "Lass, there's a man around the corner, I just feel it. And I'll be your friend, but when you meet him, I'll come second." Her voice cracked, and she closed her eyes, gathering her composure. "And that's why I've been absolutely wretched about Aldo Fiore. And why I had that little outburst with Pru, because…she'll be leavin' me, too, eventually. I'm ashamed, and I owe you both an apology."

"No, you don't. I'm the one who's on internet dating sites looking for…" She squeezed Finnie's hand. "What I have right here."

"No kissin', though." She winked.

"I can live without that." Didn't really want to, but why was she so busy trying to fill an old need in her life when she had the best friend a person could ever want right here? "But I can't live without—"

"Agnes? Is that you?"

She looked up over Finnie's head and gasped softly at the man standing behind her. Tall, silver-haired, dark-eyed, and handsome enough to take her breath away.

"Aldo?"

He laughed softly. "I thought that was you, but you know, so many people don't post their real picture. Wow. What a surprise."

She swallowed and sat up even straighter, blood thrumming in her head. "Yes, indeed. A surprise."

"May I..." He gestured toward the empty chair.

"Oh, yes, of course, I..." She finally looked at Finnie, whose eyes were wide with shock. "This is my friend," Agnes said. "Finola Kilcannon. My best friend," she added with plenty of emphasis. "We actually live together, and we're such good, happy friends that we..."

"Hello, Finola." Aldo didn't seem to notice her stuttering nonsense, but slid into the chair the Pru had left askew, and extended a hand to Finnie, then did a double take. "Well, I already know you. You're the scarf woman." He grinned at her look. "Not likely to forget those glasses."

"Oh." She touched the frames, obviously having forgotten about that disaster since it was, what? Twenty disasters ago. Twenty-one, if Agnes counted sitting face-to-face with Aldo Fiore when she was supposed to be secretly spying on him.

"Hello…again." Finnie gave him a tight smile, clearly thrown by this monkey wrench no one had seen coming.

"And you two are…" He frowned, pointing from one to the other. "Where were you when she was scarf shopping?" he asked Agnes.

"Buying…something else."

"And these little guys?" He looked down at the dogs. "Oh, these must be Pygmalion and Galatea."

He remembered her dogs' names? For some reason, that gave Agnes an unexpected thrill.

"Gala, the sensitive one," he said, giving her a little rub. "And Pyggie the…" He threw Agnes a look. "I can see why the name is a little problematic for him."

And he remembered her telling him that Pyggie was a tad overweight? "Yes." She couldn't help smiling at him and holding that delicious gaze just a few seconds too long. "That's nice that you remembered."

"These little pups need a walk," Finnie said suddenly, pushing up from the table. "You two can get to know each other in person."

"No, Finnie—"

"Nonsense, lass." She gathered the leashes and gave Aldo a quick smile, but then her natural one shone through. "'Tis nice to meet you, Mr. Fiore. You made a fine Santa up there." The very second she said that and Aldo blinked in surprise, Finnie paled. Of course she realized what she'd given away with that sentence. "I best go now!" she said brightly, hustling off with the dogs and leaving Agnes to explain.

She took a deep breath, watching Finnie walk away and bracing for something like, *You came to see me as*

Santa? and a confounded look, but he was watching Finnie, too. No, no. He was looking past her. And yes, his look was more than confounded as he stood. It was horrified.

She looked back into the mall, and her gaze landed right on...the men from the FBI, both of them staring at the current Santa, checking their phones, and looking around.

"Oh, Agnes. I'm in trouble."

No kidding.

"Can you help me?" he asked suddenly.

She fried him with a look. "Help you avoid the FBI?"

"How do you..." He dropped back on the seat. "Oh, you're in on it. You're part of...of this. What? Did you set this whole thing up? Some big, massive elaborate ruse to..." He choked softly. "What a shame."

"A shame?"

"Yes, a shame. I really liked you."

"Oh, as much as you really liked that young mother you hit up for her phone number? The one you said is 'the one.' I know your type, Aldo. Sadly, I know it all too well. It was one thing to be a moron for a man when I was eighteen, but at eighty? And, yes, I'm eighty." A little more, actually, but no need to get crazy and tell him that. "And you...you are..."

But he was shaking his head and holding up his hand. "Wait, wait. What young mother?"

"The one you flirted with when you were Santa. Got her phone number and everything."

"I got her phone number for my grandson. I'm trying like hell to find him the right woman, and after you told me that you've done some matchmaking,

I thought I might try it with all my grandkids. I was even going to ask you for some help when we had our date." He sounded genuinely sad and genuinely... *genuine.*

Could she be all wrong about him?

"What about the lady friend? The one you were shopping for when Finnie—"

"That was you!" He gave a dry, disbelieving choke. "I wanted to bring a gift to our lunch and surprise you. I wanted to..." His handsome expression formed a scowl, nothing but confusion and doubt etched on his face. "Did you come here to spy on me or to help..." He notched his head toward the men in the middle of the mall. "Them?"

"I came here because..." She glanced at Finnie, who was getting closer to the FBI agents. In a matter of seconds, they'd be over here to arrest him. And her little Aldo interlude would be over. That was fine. Finnie was right. She didn't need anyone else, but wow, it had been fun.

"Why are you here, Agnes?" he demanded.

"Because I thought I might like you, and I wanted to see you as Santa," she admitted softly. "I had no idea you were...wanted by them."

"Wanted?" He rolled his eyes. "They're not after me. They're after my sons. They just think they can bribe me to get to the real power in the operation."

She sighed. "So it's true, then. You are...that kind of man."

"What kind of man is that?"

"The kind...wanted by the FBI." She pushed up and gathered her bag. "I heard them talk about a corpse and that one of those men is carrying a ghost.

They're going to sting you with a bribe, so there. I've helped you. But that's all you'll get from me. I'm choosing my friend over…a criminal."

He just stared at her, disbelief and hurt in his eyes. "Do you always judge people so harshly, Agnes?"

She let out a sad sigh. "Yes, as a matter of fact, I do."

"Have you ever been wrong?"

"Rarely. But this time, the judgment is warranted. Goodbye, Aldo. It's been nice."

Pivoting, she walked toward the FBI men, who were already talking to Finnie. She didn't turn and look back, no matter how much she wanted to.

Why bother? No doubt he'd taken off already. But that was fine. Agnes chose Finnie, the truest friend she'd ever had. And friends were better than men anytime.

Chapter Eleven

The train started chugging along after the stop in front of Santa's Workshop, and Tor pulled them to follow it.

"He wants to run alongside it," Lucas said, jogging with the dog to let him get a little speed.

"That train is no match for him," Pru noticed as they easily kept up with the choo-choo full of kids, many with their parents folded into the undersized seats.

But Tor was determined, trotting along and making the kids turn and wave to him. He stopped at one car and sniffed and barked, then ran to catch up with it as it got away. The whole time, Lucas was threading through the crowds holding the leash, bopping back and forth to keep Tor from plowing someone down.

Finally, the train stopped right in front of the pet store, where a small crowd had gathered, including someone from a local news station with a minicam on his shoulder.

Lucas gave Pru a quick look, and they sprinted around the train to get out of the line of view. Tor pulled them to the front, where he pranced a little, his gaze alert as kids started disembarking, then a new set boarded, filling up every seat quickly.

"He's so focused on the train," Pru said.

"I know. Which makes me wonder if the puppy is on it, or was."

The whistle blew three times, and some bells chimed a familiar carol as the wheels started chugging along.

"Let me see those notes," Lucas said.

"Gramma's ideas?" She handed them over, shaking her head as she could only imagine what he'd say when he read what Gramma Finnie had written. "Brace yourself. My Gramma Finnie should come with a warning. Cuteness dead ahead."

He laughed, the chuckle coming from his chest. "No kidding. She's a living doll."

A *living doll?* She blinked at him, not at all sure what to make of that compliment, which wasn't anything she'd imagine would come out of his mouth. "Right? I adore her."

"I can see why." He glanced at the first note and smiled, flipping it up to read the next one. "How 'bout those candy canes, Pru?"

"You want one?"

He stepped back and glanced down the length of the train. "I want about thirty. And get your camera out."

"Why?" she asked as she dug out a handful of little plastic-wrapped candy canes from her backpack.

He grinned at her. "We're about to RACK up some points."

Just then, a little boy, about the age of Pru's cousin Christian, leaned out from the first train car to reach for Tor, who obliged by lowering his head for a pet.

"This is Tor," Pru said, putting her hand on the dog's head to show how friendly he was. "He's a very special dog."

"How come?" the boy asked.

"Because," Lucas said. "He's Mrs. Claus's very own dog, and he has a message and gift from her." He did a goofy little bow, then slapped a Post-it Note on the candy cane wrapper and extended it to the boy. "Good tidings from Mrs. Claus."

The little boy looked up at him, his expression saying he had no idea what *good tidings* were.

"We call them…Tor Tidings!" Lucas added, cracking Pru up as she rushed to find her phone.

"Tor Tidings, Lucas?"

"Desperate times call for desperate measures," he joked. "And let's try and look inside each car as it passes, too."

"Go ahead, Ashton," the boy's mother said when he glanced at her for permission. "Take the dog's note, and let's read it."

He took the note and candy cane, ripping into the wrapper as his mother read the note. "It says, 'Christmas in the heart puts Christmas in the air.' Aww, so sweet. Thank you!"

"Thank Tor," Lucas said. "He's spreading Christmas cheer."

The train started a slow chug, bringing the next car to Tor.

"This is *brilliant*." Pru sang the word as she stepped back to take a picture of Lucas and Tor greeting the next little girl, who reached out a grabby hand.

"I want one!" the little girl called out. "I want a Tor Tiding!"

This time, Lucas stuck the Post-it Note to the tip of Tor's nose, making the little girl release a gale of giggles as she got her candy cane, and Lucas got a look at the inside of the little car.

"Read it, Daddy!" she demanded, reaching for the note. Pru managed to get a picture right as she got the note.

"All right." Her father took the paper and cleared his throat to make it official. "'Peace on earth will come to stay when we have Christmas every day.'"

That got a little cheer from the onlookers who'd gathered to see what the extraordinary dog was doing. The next car came up to them with two little sisters in Christmas sweaters begging for their Tor Tidings from the tip of the dog's nose. Their parents read the note, and the same thing happened with the next car, and pretty soon, it was like a chorus of Christmas by kids and their parents.

"'Christmas waves a magic wand, and everything is beautiful!'"

"'Holidays are about opening our hearts, not presents!'"

"'Give hugs, not gifts!'"

"'Christmas isn't a season, it's a feeling!'"

Pru snapped a dozen pictures, then took a video of a little boy petting Tor and getting a lick, his heartfelt laughter as musical as all of Gramma Finnie's sayings being read out loud. Lucas did his very best to check each train car for the missing puppy.

As the train pulled away, they spotted the cameraman from the local TV station, walking along with one of the cars, filming the whole thing. He turned the lens to a blond woman who held a microphone and started talking.

"It's Christmas Eve at the Vestal Village Mall and—"

Just then, Tor barked and pulled Lucas toward the train, yanking on his leash.

The cameraman shot a look at them.

"He wants to run after the train," Lucas said, jogging a little to keep up with Tor.

"Just run with him." Pru gave him a nudge. "Before we end up on the evening news."

They took off with Tor, who caught up with the caboose, which had a bench running along the back car, facing backward. He batted at it with his paw, barking and trying to get on board.

With an exchange of a quick look, Pru and Lucas both shrugged, and when the train slowed to a crawl for some foot traffic ahead, they let Tor jump onto the train and climbed up after him, tucking into the tiny seat facing out to the mall.

The train picked up speed, and they just laughed while Tor got right between them, his paws on the seat, turning to look at the train cars.

"Nice RACK work!" Lucas said, looking over Tor's back at Pru. "That's gotta be worth some points."

"I'm going to submit the pictures and video right now." Pru tapped her screen, looking for the RACK IT UP app. "But weren't we supposed to find that puppy?"

"I guess Tor got a little too distracted."

After a moment, Tor gave up and stretched himself

over Pru's lap while Lucas lifted his backside onto his lap, both of them holding tight so he didn't slide off.

"And now he sleeps," Pru cracked. "The dog with no in-between mode. Off or on."

Lucas leaned back, his whole body relaxing as the dog did, resting so that his shoulder and arm pressed against Pru's. "But at least we did one random act. I know this day hasn't exactly gone as you planned."

She took a breath, the scent of leather and something very masculine filling her nose. "No, it hasn't," she admitted, smiling up at him. "But that was super creative."

"Let's see what the judges think."

She eyed the scores on her phone and let out a sigh. "Dang. Bitter Bark is in third!"

"Really? Let me see that." He put his hand on her phone, and their fingers brushed, and Pru tried not to react. At least not visibly. It was one thing to get a Christmas crush on Lucas Darling—it would be a whole new level of embarrassing if he figured it out.

"Jeez," he blinked at the phone. "Fifty points behind Sweetwater Springs and seventy behind Holly Hills. Doesn't look good for the old home team."

She leaned back in the tiny seat. "So no Winter Formal for us. Not that you probably care, but I—"

"Why wouldn't I care?" he asked.

"Oh, because you don't seem, you know..." Like the kind of guy who'd give a hoot about a dance. But then, he also didn't seem like the kind of guy who'd hand out Tor Tidings to a train full of kids. "I just didn't think you knew that many people yet."

He studied her for a moment, a little bit of a light in his eyes like he was about to say something flirtatious, but then he looked forward. "It's never easy to drop into a school in the middle of a semester."

"I would imagine," she said. "It must have been difficult leaving your old school."

"Not really. I didn't miss my school. I missed..." He let his voice trail off, looking out at the stores. "I wonder where that puppy got to."

"What do you miss?" Pru asked softly, crazy-curious about what made this complicated boy tick. Plus, it had to be that girl. Had to be.

He slid her a look. "You wouldn't believe me if I told you."

"Try me."

Waiting a beat, he let out a sigh, stroking the sleeping dog. "I wouldn't tell this to just anyone."

The butterflies that had gone dormant while they RACKed up points suddenly woke up, shook off, and dive-bombed in Pru's belly. "Oh, okay. What is it?"

"I mean, I kinda trust you." He held her gaze for a heartbeat or two. A noisy, hit-your-ribs kind of heartbeat.

"You do?" She sounded a little breathless, but couldn't really help it. Lucas made her dizzy and that was all there was to it.

"Because of them." He notched his chin in the general direction they'd come from, way back at the food court. "I can tell you have a special relationship with your grannies, so I trust you."

That made her smile. "I do, but I'm not sure why that would make you trust me."

"Because you get...that kind of relationship." He shifted in his seat for a second as if he was uncomfortable for more reasons than half an eighty-pound dog on his lap. "I miss my nanny, and if you laugh, I swear to God, Tor and I will jump off this train."

His nanny? "I'm not laughing," she said, looking hard at him. "I'm not even smiling. You have a nanny, or is that what you call your grandmother?"

"No, I mean my actual nanny. Like Mary Poppins, only imagine her older and with a thick Colombian accent. When I was little, Drina was my nanny and our housekeeper. As I got older, we just became..." He shrugged. "Like you and your Gramma Finnie. My parents, even before they split up, were never—and I do mean *never*—around. I don't have any siblings, just a few steps I can't stand. But back when I was little? It was basically me and Drina, all the time in that massive house in the hills."

"Drina. She has a pretty name."

"Had." The word came out thick, and she wasn't sure she understood. "She died."

"Oh, Lucas. I'm sorry." She put her hand on his, and for once the contact wasn't electrifying, but warm and, she hoped, comforting. "What happened?"

"She went to Florida for a vacation with her sister. While she was there, she adopted Tor, because she was nuts like that." He grinned and pet the dog, whose tail flipped when he heard his name. "Seriously, one of the most fun people I ever knew. Life was one adventure after another, and there was nothing that woman loved as much as helping other people." He stroked Tor's head. "And some dogs."

"Aww." She watched his expression soften, amazed that this gentle side of him was even more attractive than the fun, good-looking guy she'd been getting to know all day. "What happened?" she asked. "Was she sick?"

"Not at all. She was only back from Florida for a week or so, and she just…" He shook his head. "She had a stroke and died the next day."

Pru put her hand over her mouth, unable to do anything but imagine that kind of pain, closing her eyes to think of Gramma Finnie's soft hands and sweet brogue and the way she always smelled like talcum powder. "I'm so terribly sorry for you."

He swallowed noisily and nodded, clenching his jaw like he was fighting back emotion. "She was seventy-five, but really young at heart. Still cleaned my dad's house and took care of everything, but I know she wanted to retire. Wouldn't do it until I went to college, she said, otherwise I'd be alone."

Pru's heart practically shattered. "Lucas, I'm sorry for you."

"The day after Drina's funeral, my dad said he was taking Tor to a shelter. I think he knew what I'd do when he said that."

"Run away," she guessed.

"I didn't run away," he said. "That implies leaving someone who cares."

She gave his hand a squeeze, wishing she could erase the bitter tone.

"But Drina's sister was there for the funeral, Ivette Hernandez. She invited me to come to Bitter Bark and to bring Tor." He shrugged. "So I did."

"Wow," she whispered. "That's…"

He turned his hand to thread his fingers through hers and give her a warm look. "I knew I could trust you.

I know the 'my nanny died' story isn't quite the same caliber as the rumors that have been flying since I got to Bitter Bark High."

She laughed. "You do have a bad-boy look about you."

A smile pulled at his lips. "And you have a good-girl vibe."

The train stopped again, and Tor pushed up, shook off, and raised his front paws to the bench, sticking his head between them to watch the kids get off and the next set arrive, kind of blocking their view of each other, but they still held hands.

Suddenly, Tor barked and leaned forward, sniffing and letting out a soft whine.

They turned to see what had his attention, peering through the mix of kids and parents getting on board.

Tor barked again, pushing higher, trying to climb into the next car of the train.

"No, boy. No." Lucas got a hold of his collar and tried to get him down, but he resisted with his full weight, his intense gaze locked on something.

"What is it?" Pru asked, twisting completely on the caboose bench to get a better look. She grabbed his arm. "Oh my God, Lucas! Look!"

From their vantage point, they could see under the seats, and there, right in the middle, curled into a corner between two big shopping bags, was a tiny brown and white puppy.

"There he is!" they both exclaimed together just as the train started up.

Tor barked wildly, but they were moving too fast to safely jump off and run up to that car.

"Hang on, Tor." He wrapped his arm around Tor's

neck, trying to calm him. "Keep your eye on Buttercup, Pru."

"I am." She turned completely, kneeling on the bench. "Should I call out to those people sitting there?"

But she knew that would be a waste of time, because the whistle was blowing, bells were ringing on the train speaker, and the wheels and engine noise were too loud.

"They won't hear you," he said, stroking Tor's neck. "But we have him now, and we can return him to the pet store. That's all that matters."

She locked her gaze on the tiny puppy, but put her hand on top of Lucas's, resting on Tor's head. "Thanks for trusting me," she said softly. "I get the granny-nanny love. I really do."

"Thanks for not judging me."

"I figured it was an ex-girlfriend."

He snorted. "As if."

She risked taking her gaze off the dog for one second to send him a look. "Don't try to make me think you haven't had a ton of them."

He lifted a shoulder. "Think what you want. I'm picky." They held each other's gazes for a few seconds, then she heard the fake screech of brakes as the train came to a stop.

Pru turned back to the puppy…who was gone.

"No!" she cried out, squeezing the metal of the caboose back.

"Where did he go?" Lucas turned. "Does she have him?"

The woman who'd been in that car was stepping off the train with two kids in tow and multiple bags in her hand.

"Is the puppy in one of the shopping bags?"

"Maybe." Lucas stood and climbed off the little platform of the caboose, holding out his hand to Pru. "Let's follow her."

"Watch out!" she cried as three golf carts suddenly pulled up and unloaded about twenty people, all of them dressed in old-school winter garb, authentic right down to the fur muffs the women held.

"Merry Christmas!" they called out, blocking Pru and Lucas from moving as they formed a semicircle and started belting out, "God rest ye merry gentlemen, let nothing you dismay!"

But everything dismayed!

"Carolers," Lucas muttered, trying to see past them to the woman with the bags. "Seriously?"

They tried to move left, then right, around the singers, but already a crowd of onlookers had gathered, essentially forming a human roadblock across the mall. Precious seconds ticked away as Tor pulled one way, then the other, and the puppy got farther and farther away.

"Get back on the train!" Pru said, scrambling toward the caboose as it started to move. "They have to let it through!"

They managed to climb back on just as the train picked up speed, and the crowd broke to let it through. It was the perfect solution, but the whole thing took so long, they couldn't find the woman with the bags anywhere in the crowd.

"Keep looking," Pru said, standing to scan every person. "She had light hair and a navy jacket."

"Like fifty million other people," Lucas replied, peering into the crowds.

"Hey. It's Christmas. Anything's possible."

"Wait! Is that her?" He pointed toward the wide opening of another department store a good fifty yards away at a blonde with two kids, many bags, and a navy jacket.

"Maybe. Hard to tell."

"Let's give it a shot. You want to wait here?" he asked.

Pru hesitated for a nanosecond. "Not a chance."

Lucas jumped off first, and Tor followed, then Pru leaped off, caught her balance, and laughed. "Get that puppy!"

"Did you hear that, Tor? Permission to run and get that puppy! Run!" He unclipped the leash, and Tor took off like a bolt of lightning, and all they could do was hold hands and run after him, left in the greyhound's dust.

Chapter Twelve

Agnes's heart thumped as she walked toward the FBI men deep in conversation with Finnie. She'd done the right thing, hadn't she? She'd learned her lesson as a young girl about letting a handsome man lead her astray, right? This wasn't the dumbest thing she'd ever done, was it?

Because Aldo sure seemed...*nice.*

"He's right there," Finnie said, turning to point and aiming directly at Agnes. "Oh, lass. 'Tis you."

"He was there," Agnes said. "But I'm sure he's gone by now."

The big man looked past her. "No, he's there."

He was? She spun around, surprised to see Aldo still sitting at the table, leaning back, his arms crossed, a smug smile on his face. "I thought he'd run."

Good Lord, had she misjudged him?

"Is Aldo a friend of yours, ma'am?" the other man—Sammy, if she recalled correctly—asked.

A friend? He could have been, she thought, tearing her gaze from his. "Not really. I suppose he's tired of running from you guys."

Sammy let out a frustrated sigh. "Look, Big Mike

124

and I can be awfully persistent, but we're not getting anywhere with him at all. Maybe you could help us out?"

Finnie gasped softly. "'Tisn't likely we'll get in the middle of this." She slipped her arm around Agnes's. "Come on, before we get shot."

"Shot?" Sammy snorted a laugh. "We're not that determined to get the business, ma'am."

Finnie was pulling her away, but Agnes stood firm, turning to him. "To get the business? Is that a code word for bringing in a wanted criminal?"

The two men stared at her, then at each other, then at her again. "Pardon me?" they asked in perfect unison.

Another little thread of discomfort pulled at her heart. "A wanted criminal," she said, a little louder this time. "You're with the FBI, and he's..." She glanced over her shoulder, and sure enough, he was still there, folding a piece of paper as he watched her, that semi-amused smile still pulling at his lips.

"He's what?" one of them asked.

He's...handsome, she thought glumly. Agnes pushed the thought away and turned back. "He's a wanted criminal, right? You found a corpse? I assume he's responsible."

Sammy's face suddenly tightened like he was trying to hold himself back from saying something. Of course an FBI agent wouldn't want to give anything away.

"Actually, I think one of his sons is the culprit," the other man said. "We've been looking for the corpse for a long time."

Agnes shook her head, the words sickening to her.

"This is not a family I want to get involved with. Come on, Finnie."

But this time, Finnie was the one standing her ground. She looked from one man to the other, then back at Aldo, who hadn't moved. "What exactly is he guilty of?" she asked.

"Guilty?" Big Mike looked confused. "It's not exactly a *crime*."

"Murder isn't a crime?" Agnes demanded. "Since when?"

Once again, the two men shared a look, and the only thing Sammy was holding back now was laughter, which came bubbling out of him.

"Murder?" Big Mike asked, barely able to choke out the word.

"And isn't that a gun in your jacket pocket?" Agnes said, her voice rising with tension.

Next to her, Finnie squeezed her arm. "Um, Agnes, I'm starting to think…"

"You really think Aldo Fiore could kill a guy?" Sammy asked, laughing so hard he had to wipe a tear from his eye. "Did you hear that, Mike?"

But Mike just shook his head, also laughing.

"Agnes, maybe we jumped to the wrong conclusion."

Without answering Finnie, Agnes turned for another look at Aldo. He was leaning forward now, his chin resting on his knuckles, staring at her. The smile had faded, and his expression was just wistful. Maybe sad.

"So…" Agnes turned to the men. "You're not with the FBI, and that's not a gun in your pocket, and there isn't a corpse?"

Mike threw his head back and let out a hearty laugh. "We are with FBI," he said. "But not *the* FBI..."

Sammy reached into his pocket, and both women drew back a little, but he only produced a business card, handing it to Agnes.

"Sam Robinson, owner of Flowers and Blooms, Incorporated. It's a small nursery, trying to grow. I've been after the Fiore & Sons landscaping business for a long time. They buy the most product and could really help our bottom line."

Oh dear. Agnes stared at him. Finnie let out a soft moan.

"And this?" Mike reached into the bulky pocket and pulled out a container wrapped in tissue, which he peeled back to reveal a small white flower unlike anything Agnes had ever seen. "This is a ghost orchid, one of the rarest blooms in the world."

"Pretty," Finnie said.

"We're the only nursery in five hundred miles that can grow it." Sammy beamed with pride. "Aldo's son, Tony, who does want to do business with us, told us if we offered this to Aldo, he might come around and add us to his list of very exclusive vendors."

"So, the ghost orchid is a...bribe." Agnes slowly lifted a hand to her mouth to cover the string of very bad words threatening to tumble out.

"We like to think of it as an invitation to do business together," Sammy said.

"And the corpse?" Finnie asked, her own voice sounding reed-thin.

"Wow." Big Mike stifled a laugh. "You two are some impressive spies."

"But what about the dead body?" Finnie stepped closer, straightening the glasses that refused to sit right on her face.

Sammy drew back, then nodded. "The corpse is another of the rarest plants in the world. One of our guys was at a landscape job that Fiore & Sons did, and they had one. If they were able to get a corpse, then they must have signed an exclusive deal with our biggest competitors, which is bad for us. Very bad."

"'Cause Fiore & Sons is the absolute best landscaping company in the county. They get the biggest jobs and make the most money," Mike added. "The whole family is highly regarded, but Aldo, well. He's like…"

"Aldo's the most respected man in his business," Sammy finished for him. "He's fair, smart, pays on time, treats everyone like family, and well, he always plays Santa at the mall. How can you not love a guy like that?"

Agnes pressed her fingers to her lips, his words coming back to her…

Do you always judge people so harshly, Agnes?

She wanted to turn one more time, but simply didn't have the nerve. She was too ashamed.

"So, if you know the guy, maybe you can help us." Mike held out the ghost orchid. "Give him this and put in a good word for FBI. Not *the* FBI, but…" He smiled. "We're just an up-and-coming business and would love for his company to buy our products. It's that simple."

Finnie bit her lip and took the plant. "A ghost orchid. Well, that's a new one on me, lad."

"Thanks for your help, ladies," Sammy said.

"Merry Christmas!" With a nod, Mike glanced over Agnes's shoulder to where they'd been sitting at the food court. He shrugged and smiled, then the two men walked away, rounding the Christmas tree without looking back.

"Agnes," Finnie whispered.

"I know, I know. We're idiots. Fools. Conclusion jumpers. What can I do?"

"Nothing." Finnie patted her arm and turned them both toward the food court. "He's gone."

Disappointment whipped through her. And regret. And frustration. And one little kick of *what the hell was I thinking listening to Finnie Kilcannon?*

"He left something on the table, Agnes." Finnie gave a nudge. "What is that?"

Agnes shifted her attention to the empty table, seeing something white and folded on the surface. "The missing puppy flyer?" Frowning and hating herself for hoping it was more a note of forgiveness?—she led the way back to where they'd been sitting.

Yes, that was the flyer, but the paper was intricately folded into the shape of a long-stemmed flower.

"A rose," Finnie whispered.

"Oh." Agnes let out a little moan. "Just like Nik."

"In what way?" Finnie asked.

She smiled, surprised that tears welled up. "The day he came to my home to tell my parents he didn't care what I'd done, that I would be his wife, he brought roses from the florist shop where he worked. And every year on the anniversary of that very day, he gave me a rose."

"And now you have a paper one." Finnie lifted it and handed it to Agnes. "What do you think that means?"

Agnes closed her eyes and dropped into the empty seat. "That I misjudged him."

"We both did," Finnie said, sliding into the next seat, taking off her crooked glasses so Agnes could see her gaze was direct and sincere. "I assumed the worst, believed old rumors, and did my level best to keep you from happiness because I was afraid of bein' alone." The confession came out raw and real, in thick brogue that reached in and tore Agnes's heart out.

"Which is a testament to what a good friend you are," Agnes said softly, laying two hands on her friend's arm. "What's a rose when you have a four-leaf clover?"

Finnie's little frown formed. "Not followin' ye, lass."

"I believe I've seen a little stitching on the shelf that says, 'A good friend is like a four-leaf clover…'"

"'Hard to find and lucky to have,'" Finnie whispered. "Are you forgivin' me, then, Agnes?"

She smiled and gave Finnie's arm a squeeze. "'Tis Christmas, lassie," Agnes said in a seriously bad imitation of a brogue. "I'll be forgivin' you."

Finnie laughed, even though it was obvious she didn't want to. "What a pair we are," she mused, reaching down to pet Gala, who sat between them, her little head going back and forth as she followed the rhythm of the conversation and, knowing Gala, the heart of it, too.

Agnes looked down and twirled the paper rose,

noticing some writing on one of the petals. She stared at it, then looked up at Finnie, her eyes wide.

"A note?" Finnie asked.

Agnes lifted the petal to try to read, but all she could see was a few words...*Christmas to you.*

"It's just 'Merry Christmas,'" she said, a little disappointed. "And frankly, after how we misjudged him, that's being generous."

"Are you sure that's all it says?"

She examined the flower, but the words disappeared under an elaborate fold. "I'd have to take it apart and ruin it to read the rest." She brought it to her nose as if it had an actual scent, smiling at Finnie. "And I honestly would like to keep this as it is. A reminder not to judge so harshly."

Finnie's eyes welled up. "Oh, Agnes."

"Hey, fuhgedaboudit, as Aldo and his hit men would say."

But Finnie didn't laugh. She shook her head, and one of those tears escaped.

"Seriously, Finn, don't—"

"Agnes." She reached out and wrapped her gnarled little fingers around Agnes's hand. "Do you realize how far you've come? How much you've changed? How soft and sweet and forgiving you've become? No one can ever accuse my Agnes of having sharp edges."

Against her will, Agnes felt her own eyes fill. "Oh, Finnie. Thank you."

"'Tis true. You're a sweet woman, and don't let anyone ever say different."

"It's not that, which is nice, but..." She swallowed the lump in her throat. "I like being 'your Agnes.'"

"Well, you are. Like it or not. I'm afraid I wrecked your romance."

"No, you didn't. You changed my life."

They held hands for a moment, both smiling through tears as Gala slid to the floor and let out a contented whine.

Chapter Thirteen

Somehow, the lady with the bags and two kids moved like she was on roller skates. At least it felt that way as Pru and Lucas followed Tor on a tear into Dillard's. The crowds parted for him, but some of the people yelled at Pru and Lucas as they passed. A few people laughed. But most jumped out of the way to avoid what might first look like a runaway horse.

He raced into Dillard's, ruffled a rack of sweaters, zipped right through a family of shoppers, and bumped a mannequin that Lucas grabbed seconds before she toppled.

"Hey!" a saleswoman hollered at them.

"Sorry, ma'am," Lucas said quickly, then looked at the mannequin. "You, too, lady."

Pru bit her lip and kept running after Tor, trying to watch the woman with the bags and kids as she passed the lingerie section.

"Stop!" she yelled, as much at the woman as the dog.

She did pause, but only to glance at some handbags, which was long enough for her to realize a dog was running at her. She let out a little shriek, dropped her bags, grabbed her kids, and Lucas vaulted ahead and managed to snag Tor before he launched himself at the lady.

"You have a puppy!" Lucas cried out, forgoing any explanation.

"In your bag," Pru added, breathless, pointing to the largest paper shopping bag, from Old Navy. Just then, it wiggled, wobbled, and fell to its side.

"Mommy, look!"

Out scrambled the baby basset, who paused in surprise just long enough for Tor to let out a furious bark. Then the puppy took off like a shot, tripped over one of her ears, rolled once, and popped up. Then she right darted into lingerie and hid under a rack of robes.

Lucas and Tor followed, while Pru offered a smile to the woman. "She got in your bag on the train," she explained, looking over her shoulder. "We're trying to get her back to the pet store."

"I want that puppy, Mommy!" her little girl called out.

The mother looked a little shell-shocked at the whole situation, pulling both kids back. "But you can't have it, honey," she managed to say, her gaze on Pru. "Please tell her."

"I'm sorry," Pru said, slowing to look down at the child. "That's Buttercup. And she already has an owner, and they are very upset that she's lost."

The little girl opened her mouth to wail, but her mother dropped down to console her, so Pru rushed toward Lucas, who was doing his best to hold on to Tor.

"Where is she?" she asked.

He nodded toward a round table laden with bras of every imaginable size. "Under the underwear."

"I'll get her." She flew to the table, lifted the skirt, and the minute she did, Buttercup shot out with a pathetic little bark and a roll over the carpet. Pru reached for her, but Tor was faster, breaking free from Lucas and diving toward the little dog.

For a moment, they all froze, but Tor gently eased his teeth over the back of the puppy's neck, lifting her tenderly like a prize.

"You got the puppy, Tor!" Lucas exclaimed. "Quick, Pru. Get a picture. That's gotta be worth some RACK points."

Her heart practically folded that he cared about her silly contest when there were so many other problems at hand, but she did manage to get a shot or two, then a ten-second video as Tor took a few steps, and some shoppers gathered around the underwear displays and started to clap.

"Feliz naughty dog," one of them sang out, making everyone laugh.

"Feliz naughty dog," someone else sang in the same tune, getting another cheer, so loud it made the puppy squirm, so Pru reached down to ease her out of Tor's mouth.

"You are not a naughty dog," she cooed in Buttercup's ear. "And neither are you, Tor." She petted his head and smiled up at Lucas. "You want to take this little girl back to The Animal House?"

"As quickly and quietly as possible." He tugged Tor's leash and brought him close to nuzzle his head, but his gaze stayed on Pru. "Did you get those bras in the photo?"

Her eyes widened, and she looked back at the table. "I might have. Why?"

He shrugged, some merriment in his dark eyes. "Might give a new meaning to RACK it up."

She cracked up, waving to the small crowd and snuggling Buttercup close to her.

They were still smiling when they made their way back to the pet store, forced to stop for the carolers, let the train go by, and pause for shoppers to coo over Tor and the puppy. For his part, the greyhound never veered far from Buttercup, sniffing occasionally and licking her little ears.

When they reached the pet store, the same woman stood at the entry, but this time, they weren't greeted with a warm hello. Her scowl shifted to a shocked gasp when she saw Buttercup in Pru's arms.

"David!" she called into the store. "They're returning him! They've surrendered Buttercup."

Surrendered? Pru shot her a look, taking a breath to launch a defense, but Lucas put a hand on her shoulder.

"Don't sweat it, Pru. Let's just get the dog back and get out of here."

"There he is!" The manager, David, pointed right at Lucas, and the man with a camera on his shoulder swung around. "That's the boy that caused all this trouble. And his dog."

"Wait a sec—"

But Lucas added some pressure to quiet Pru. "Just give them the dog. Tor and I will stay outside."

Before she could argue, he backed away, using his strength to guide Tor out of the store.

"That's right," David called after him. "Slink off, puppy thief."

A jolt of indignation rocked Pru. "He's not a puppy thief!"

David just rolled his eyes as he came around the counter. "Let me have her." He reached out to grab Buttercup, and she instinctively backed up to protect the puppy.

"Be gentle," she warned.

"Oh, that's rich," David snorted. "After what you and your loser boyfriend put us through today."

"He's not a loser." Fury straightened her back, and something even more powerful made her turn to the camera, knowing it was trained on her and, if that red light meant anything, recording. "He's a great kid who spent his entire day trying to perform dozens of Random Acts of Christmas Kindness, including running through this mall trying to find a puppy who, I must say, should have been better protected."

"Excuse me?" David spat the question.

"He should have been," Pru said, speaking to the camera lens. "I speak from knowledge, since my grandfather and all my uncles run a canine rescue and training center, my mom's a vet, and my dad trains therapy dogs." The authority rolled off her tongue, spurred on by just how wrong this situation was. "Those puppies were being held in a flimsy pen that a child could knock over, and frankly, this store is lucky they didn't lose more. It was pet negligence, actually, and they should be cited."

"Okay, little budding lawyer, that's enough." He held out his hands. "Give me Buttercup, and go have your Christmas, kid. You've caused enough problems, and we don't need any more."

Before she handed Buttercup to the manager, she

gave a comforting stroke to the little dog's head and playfully flipped her long ears. "I hope you're going somewhere wonderful, little angel," she whispered.

As she gave up the puppy, something moved in her peripheral vision, and she turned to see the reporter who'd been talking to the camera earlier.

"What do you mean you've been performing Random Acts of Christmas Kindness?" the woman asked, coming closer with her microphone in hand. "That's intriguing."

"It's a county-wide contest," Pru explained. "And we're here representing Bitter Bark High School."

"Really? Can you tell me more?"

"I will," Pru promised. "But if you do a story, can you please include my friend and his dog? This isn't about me. The manager of this store has unfairly judged him and blamed him for something he didn't do. In fact, this puppy could be halfway to who knows where if not for those two."

The woman frowned, glancing outside. "Is he the boy handing out the candy canes and cute little sayings with the handsome racing dog?"

"Yes, that's them. Tor Tidings!"

She chuckled. "Okay, let's go talk to both of you. Would you mind being on the six o'clock news?"

"Not at all," Pru said, unable to resist throwing a *take that* look at David, who was, to his credit, giving Buttercup a treat. "Hey, David," she called. When he looked up, she added a smile. "Merry Christmas!"

His response was slow and a little grudging, but even Scrooge had to nod. "Happy Holidays, young lady." Then a smile grew. "You really should go to law school."

She laughed as they walked out of the pet store, and she was a little surprised to see Gramma Finnie and Yiayia talking to Lucas.

"Is the Santa stalking all done?" she asked under her breath as she brought the reporter over.

"'Tis done, lass." Gramma Finnie gave Yiayia a look Pru didn't quite understand, but she was used to these two speaking in a secret, silent language. And she didn't even want to ask about the plant Gramma Finnie was holding. "And I understand Tor saved the day."

"He had some help from Pru," Lucas added graciously.

"And this fine lad has agreed to have Christmas Eve dinner with us at Waterford Farm tonight." Gramma Finnie beamed with the news that somehow didn't surprise Pru at all. Thrill? Yes. Surprise? Not a bit.

"You okay with that?" he asked Pru quickly. "Because if you've had enough of me and Tor..."

"Oh, no. I mean, yes. Have dinner with the whole family. And if you think we're crazy, wait until you see the Irish drink and the Greeks dance. And that's before Midnight Mass, which of course, you can skip—"

"I'd love to go."

She blinked at him, one hundred percent certain that the very last thing she could have dreamed would happen tonight would be Lucas Darling accompanying her whole family to Midnight Mass. "Really?"

He smiled and leaned closer, whispering in her ear, "I went every year with Drina."

"You did? Well, then, this is perfect. You can go with us, and Tor will be well taken care of in the luxury kennels of Waterford Farm."

Before he could answer, the reporter got right in front of him with her microphone. "Young man, could you tell us what this RACK IT UP program is all about?"

"Sure, but this girl here is the one who organized it." He put his arm around Pru, and they faced the camera together.

"Is this your girlfriend?" the reporter asked.

"Um..." He looked down at her. "Not yet." He added a secret wink, and all the butterflies went flat-out crazy.

Chapter Fourteen

Waterford Farm never looked merrier than it did when completely decked out for a family Christmas Eve. Agnes couldn't help but admire the creative designs and festive decorations done by the woman who'd once been married to Agnes's dearly departed son, Nico. No longer Katie Santorini, she was now Finnie's daughter-in-law, married to Daniel Kilcannon.

"You having fun, Yiayia?" Katie asked, pausing on her way to the kitchen. "You look a little glum for Christmas Eve."

Yiayia managed a smile. "I'm fine, Katie." She reached out and put a hand on the other woman's arm. "Merry Christmas, sweetie."

Katie's eyes flickered. No doubt she was taken aback by the endearment, what with the acrimonious relationship they'd had as mother-in-law and daughter-in-law. "Merry Christmas, Yiayia."

With another smile, Agnes glanced around, her gaze landing on Finnie, who sat on the sofa in the massive family room, with Gala on her lap and Pyggie at her f

Agnes joined her, petting both dogs after she set her drink on the coffee table.

"I saw ye chattin' with Katie," Finnie said.

"She said I look glum. It's just the Botox won't let me smile."

Finnie snorted a laugh. "You don't need that poison, lass." She leaned closer to whisper over the family commotion, "Are ye thinkin' about him?"

"Actually, no," Agnes said. "I was thinking about this incredible Kilcannon and Mahoney and Santorini family that you and I preside over."

"Shall we start planning our next match, then? I mean, if it's not going to be you?"

Agnes chuckled. "It was never going to be me."

"Are ye sure you're not too disappointed about Aldo?"

"I'm sure, Finnie." She reached for her ouzo and waited for Finnie to get her shot of Jameson's. "To the very best friend I've ever had. Merry Christmas, Finola."

"Merry Christmas, Agnes."

Just as their glasses clinked, a cheer went up from a group gathered around the television. Agnes and Finnie got a little closer to see through the crowd that formed a big semicircle in front of the large flat screen.

"Here we go!" Molly, Pru's mother, shifted her young Danny from one hip to the other, her eyes bright. "It's on now!"

A hush fell over the room as the local news anchor troduced the story with the words on the screen ing *Mall Madness Leads to Kindness!* That earned her big cheer from the family.

"While many people love to brag about being finished with their Christmas shopping in November," the reporter said, "the crowds at Vestal Village Mall today proved that's not the case for everyone. And what a treat those folks had today, courtesy of two local teenagers and one rambunctious greyhound who saved a lost puppy and brought smiles to dozens of faces."

Another cheer, and Agnes leaned a little to the right to see past two of her tall grandsons to where Lucas and Pru stood, sharing a quick glance. Maybe not so quick. That was definitely *extended* eye contact.

"Oh, Finnie, look," she whispered, putting an arm around her friend's narrow shoulders to ease her closer so she could see. "Look at their hands."

Their knuckles touched, then Lucas slyly curled his fingers around Pru's hand, secretly holding it as the story continued, the camera zooming in on one of Finnie's Christmas notes stuck to Tor's nose, to the delight of a little boy.

"Look at your work on TV, Finn."

"Look at your work holding hands, Agnes." She dropped her snowy white head on Agnes's shoulder. "The Dogmothers strike again."

Yet another cheer interrupted them as the reporter showered Bitter Bark High School students with praise for their efforts and told the audience that the winner of the RACK IT UP contest would be announced later tonight. Also, the local TV station would be covering the Winter Formal that the winning school would be enjoying in January.

"That winning school won't be us," Pru told t'

143

all after the story was finished, and the cheering quieted. "The final tally is in already." She waved her phone and shrugged. "Holly Hills beat us by forty points, but we came in second. Sadly, no dance for second place."

"But Bitter Bark came out smelling like a rose," Molly said as the group began to break up into smaller conversations.

"Speaking of roses." Agnes reached to the table next to her, where she'd placed her origami flower from a man whose last name meant flower. "I do have this little gift to appreciate."

Finnie took it from her and twirled it. "'Tis very telling, this rose."

"Telling of what?"

"It says something about a man with the patience and skill to do something like this. And so fast and secretly." She winked. "Bet he's good with his hands."

"Finola!" Agnes waved her hand with a laugh at the very second Finnie used the paper rose to underscore her meaning. In a flash, Agnes's long nail caught one of the petals and accidentally unfolded it. "Oh!"

"I'm so sorry!" Finnie exclaimed as the flower fanned open and lost its shape. "Agnes, how clumsy of me!"

"No, no, it was my fault."

"See?" Finnie looked at her. "You're a changed woman, Agnes."

"Hush!" she said on a laugh as she fingered the ruined origami. "I'll lose all my power in this family if they're not scared of…" Her voice trailed off as she looked at the paper. "Finnie. I can read what he wrote now."

Finnie sat up, excited, then took off her glasses—

the good ones that weren't crooked. "Here. You'll need to borrow these."

Agnes slid them on and smoothed the page to read what Aldo Fiore had written.

When you're ready for romance, call me. I promise I'll be in the garden and not in jail. Aldo

She read the words again and again, soaking them up. "What does this mean?" she whispered.

Finnie snorted a laugh. "It means he is forgiving, romantic, patient, and has a sense of humor."

That made Agnes smile.

"It also means he'll make a very nice boyfriend…if that's what you want."

"I don't know what I want," Agnes admitted, fanning herself with the paper. "But I don't hate the idea of finding out." She turned and looked down at Finnie. "As long as you know that you can never, ever be replaced."

"I know." Finnie patted her arm and jutted her chin toward the door as Pru and Lucas, hand in hand, stepped outside into the chilly night where the very first snowflakes danced in the beam of the porch light. "But I do believe the Dogmothers are about to see a little less of that lass in the coming days."

When they disappeared out the door, at least half of the family turned to Finnie and Agnes with wide eyes and questioning looks, none more intense than Molly's and Trace's.

"What exactly happened at that mall today?" Molly asked them.

"You saw the news report, lass," Finnie said.

Trace put his arm around Molly. "And we just saw our daughter holding hands with a boy."

"A very nice boy," Agnes said. "With a good heart."

"He does seem nice," Molly agreed. "But…"

"Don't judge him by his looks," Finnie warned, pointing a playful finger at Trace. "If we'd have been counting tattoos instead of your fine qualities, lad, would you even be standing here today?"

Over the laughter, Trace conceded that with a tip of his head. "You're right, Gramma. But she's so young."

"And has her head on straighter than some people three times her age," Agnes said. "Let her have a little fun, Dad."

"We are," Molly assured them. "We were just wondering how this happened."

Finnie and Agnes high-fived. "Well, we are the Dogmothers."

As the family reacted with laughter and rolled eyes, Agnes turned to look out the window, past a candle, to where Pru and Lucas stood on the covered patio, facing each other as Lucas helped her slide into his leather jacket.

Watching them for a moment, she leaned in to whisper to Finnie, "I wonder if they know they're under the mistletoe."

Pru snuggled into the butter-soft leather, the smell already deeply embedded in her memory bank, where she'd surely call it up many nights so she could remember this one. She looked up at Lucas, finally used to the insane thrill that being this close to him sent over her whole body.

"So, now you've met them all. The Kilcannons, Mahoneys, and Santorinis," she said. "That's my crew."

"And the Bancrofts," he added.

"Oh, yeah. I always forget we have a different last name."

"Your dad is so cool. I loved the way he handled Tor when we took him into the kennel."

"I told you, he's amazing with dogs. He could make Tor a therapy dog."

"He already is," Lucas said, glancing toward the kennels. "Helped heal me, mostly."

Pru smiled, rubbing the leather. "And now he's the most famous dog in Vestal Valley County," she said, studying Lucas's face for a minute, not even trying to hide how much she liked to look at it. After all, he was kind of looking at her the exact same way.

"What is it?" she asked on a laugh when the mutual studying seemed to go on a few seconds past comfortable.

"I was just wondering."

"Wondering what?"

"How come you didn't have a bunch of friends to go RACKing with today. You're pretty popular, and I'm surprised a girl like you ended up alone."

She was getting used to the fact that he'd been noticing her since he'd arrived at Bitter Bark High, but the idea still gave her a little shiver of satisfaction.

"They have boyfriends," she said simply, "and decided to spend the day with them."

"But you don't?"

She bit her lip, eyeing him, remembering what he'd said to the reporter when she'd asked if Pru wa his girlfriend. *Not yet.* "No," she said softly. "Wanna know the truth?"

"Always."

"I've never had a boyfriend, and I've never been—"

"Pru." The door burst open, and her mom was there, holding out Pru's phone. "Your phone's blowing up. Do you want it?"

She wasn't sure if the interruption was on purpose, but she and Mom would talk about it all later in great detail, she had no doubt. "Sure," she said, stepping away from Lucas to get the phone. "Thanks, Mom. We'll be back in soon. Did we start the presents?"

"It'll be a while until we start unwrapping. But you don't want to miss Gramma Finnie lighting the candle in the living room window and telling us how the Irish invite strangers."

Pru laughed and glanced at Lucas. "Honestly, you do not want to miss that."

"I don't," he agreed.

When Mom closed the door, Pru lifted her phone and tapped the screen, doing a little double take at the long list of texts. "Whoa. It is blowing…holy cow."

"What? Is everything okay?"

"Lucas!" She looked up at him, practically dancing. "We won! Bitter Bark High won the RACK IT UP contest!"

"I thought the points were counted already."

"One of the judges saw the news!" She grabbed his arm and gave a squeeze. "They gave us fifty points for the Tor Tidings and saving the puppy!"

"Really?" He seemed as genuinely excited as she was. "We won? We really won?"

"Because of you!"

"Because of us," he added, putting his arms around her for a celebratory hug. Maybe a celebratory hug. Maybe just…an embrace. "And Tor."

"Feliz naughty dog." Laughter bubbled up as she let him pull her in a little closer and looked up into his eyes.

"You know what this means, don't you?"

That she might actually melt like those first few snowflakes floating through the air. "What does it mean?"

"We're having a Winter Formal."

"I guess we are."

He added a little pressure, leaving no doubt that this was an embrace, not just a friendly hug. "And I bet your friends are going with their boyfriends again."

She tried to breathe, but honestly? It wasn't easy. "Yeah, they will."

"Then why don't you go with yours?"

Forget breathing, she couldn't even think for a second. "Mine."

"Prudence Bancroft…" He dipped his head a little closer, letting that stray lock of dark hair fall over his brow. "Would you go to the Winter Formal with me?"

She gave in to another shiver, and he had to have felt it. "Yes, Lucas Darling, I would like to do that."

He smiled, not making any move to let go of her. "Now what were you going to tell me before your mom came out? You've never had a boyfriend, and you've never been…what?"

"You know." She closed her eyes with a soft laugh.

"Then look up." He pointed above them, and she lifted her face to see the green cluster of leaves with a

149

red ribbon hanging from the patio covering. "I saw it on the way in," he admitted.

"And that's why you wanted to come outside and see the snowfall?"

He closed a little bit of the space between their faces, holding her gaze. "Yes," he said quietly right before his lips brushed hers in the softest, sweetest, most perfect first kiss she could have ever imagined.

"Wow. Was that another Random Act of Christmas Kindness?" she asked breathlessly.

"The first of many more, I hope." He gave a sly smile. "Let's go tell Tor we won."

Laughing, they stepped out into the snowflakes, arm in arm.

Want to know the next Dogmothers release date and see the cover? Sign up for the newsletter at www.roxannestclaire.com.

Or get daily updates, sneak peeks, and insider information at the Dogfather Reader Facebook Group! The Dogmothers get all the news first and a front row seat on the writing process for the whole series!

www.facebook.com/groups/roxannestclairereaders/

The Dogmothers is a spinoff series of
The Dogfather

Available Now

SIT...STAY...BEG (Book 1)

NEW LEASH ON LIFE (Book 2)

LEADER OF THE PACK (Book 3)

SANTA PAWS IS COMING TO TOWN (Book 4)
(A Holiday Novella)

BAD TO THE BONE (Book 5)

RUFF AROUND THE EDGES (Book 6)

DOUBLE DOG DARE (Book 7)

BARK! THE HERALD ANGELS SING (Book 8)
(A Holiday Novella)

OLD DOG NEW TRICKS (Book 9)

Join the private Dogfather Reader Facebook Group!

www.facebook.com/groups/roxannestclairereaders/

When you join, you'll find inside info on all the books and characters, sneak peeks, and a place to share the love of tails and tales!

The Dogmothers Series

Available Now

HOT UNDER THE COLLAR (Book 1)

THREE DOG NIGHT (Book 2)

DACHSHUND THROUGH THE SNOW (Book 3)
(A Holiday Novella)

CHASING TAIL (Book 4)

HUSH, PUPPY (Book 5)

MAN'S BEST FRIEND (Book 6)

FELIZ NAUGHTY DOG (Book 7)
(A Holiday Novella)

and many more to come!

For a complete list, buy links, and reading order of all my books, visit www.roxannestclaire.com. Be sure to sign up for my newsletter to find out when the next book is released!

A Dogfather/Dogmothers Family Reference Guide

THE KILCANNON FAMILY

Daniel Kilcannon aka *The Dogfather*
Son of Finola (Gramma Finnie) and Seamus Kilcannon. Married to Annie Harper for 36 years until her death. Veterinarian, father, and grandfather. Widowed at opening of series. Married to Katie Santorini (*Old Dog New Tricks*) with dogs Rusty and Goldie.

The Kilcannons (from oldest to youngest):

• **Liam** Kilcannon and Andi Rivers (*Leader of the Pack*) with Christian and Fiona and dog, Jag

• **Shane** Kilcannon and Chloe Somerset (*New Leash on Life*) with daughter Annabelle and dogs, Daisy and Ruby

• **Garrett** Kilcannon and Jessie Curtis (*Sit...Stay... Beg*) with son Patrick and dog, Lola

• **Molly** Kilcannon and Trace Bancroft (*Bad to the Bone*) with daughter Pru and son Danny and dog, Meatball

• **Aidan** Kilcannon and Beck Spencer (*Ruff Around the Edges*) with dog, Ruff

• **Darcy** Kilcannon and Josh Ranier (*Double Dog Dare*) with dogs, Kookie and Stella

THE MAHONEY FAMILY

Colleen Mahoney

Daughter of Finola (Gramma Finnie) and Seamus Kilcannon and younger sister of Daniel. Married to Joe Mahoney for a little over 10 years until his death. Owner of Bone Appetit (canine treat bakery) and mother.

The Mahoneys (from oldest to youngest):

• **Declan** Mahoney and Evie Hewitt (*Man's Best Friend*) with dog Judah
• **Connor** Mahoney and Sadie Hartman (*Chasing Tail*) with dog, Frank, and cat, Demi
• **Braden** Mahoney and **Cassie** Santorini (*Hot Under the Collar*) with dogs, Jelly Bean and Jasmine

• **Ella** Mahoney and...

THE SANTORINI FAMILY

Katie Rogers Santorini

Dated **Daniel** Kilcannon in college and introduced him to Annie. Married to Nico Santorini for forty years until his death two years after Annie's. Interior Designer and mother. Recently married to **Daniel** Kilcannon (*Old Dogs New Tricks*).

The Santorinis

• **Nick** Santorini and...

• **John** Santorini (identical twin to Alex) and Summer Jackson (*Hush, Puppy*) with daughter Destiny and dog, Maverick

• **Alex** Santorini (identical twin to John) and Grace Donovan (*Three Dog Night*) with dogs, Bitsy, Gertie and Jack

• **Theo** Santorini and…

• **Cassie** Santorini and **Braden** Mahoney (*Hot Under the Collar*) with dogs, Jelly Bean and Jasmine

Katie's mother-in-law from her first marriage, **Agnes "Yiayia" Santorini,** now lives in Bitter Bark with **Gramma Finnie** and their dachshunds, Pygmalion (Pyggie) and Galatea (Gala). These two women are known as "The Dogmothers."

About The Author

Published since 2003, Roxanne St. Claire is a *New York Times* and *USA Today* bestselling author of more than fifty romance and suspense novels. She has written several popular series, including The Dogfather, The Dogmothers, Barefoot Bay, the Guardian Angelinos, and the Bullet Catchers.

In addition to being a ten-time nominee and one-time winner of the prestigious RITA™ Award for the best in romance writing, Roxanne has won the National Readers' Choice Award for best romantic suspense four times. Her books have been published in dozens of languages and optioned for film.

A mother of two but recent empty-nester, Roxanne lives in Florida with her husband and her two dogs, Ginger and Rosie.

www.roxannestclaire.com
www.twitter.com/roxannestclaire
www.facebook.com/roxannestclaire
www.roxannestclaire.com/newsletter/

Made in the USA
Las Vegas, NV
07 September 2022

54859905R00100